BEER
FOR MY
CORPSES

BEER FOR MY CORPSES

THE PICK'S POCKET SERIES

C.M. MCGUIRE

<u>Anthology</u>

Last Night at the Jolly Chicken

<u>Misplaced Mercenaries</u> by Kevin Pettway

A Good Running Away

Blow Out the Candle When You Leave

Big Damn Magic

Illusions of Decency

Heroes Kill Everyone

<u>Hettie Stormheart series</u> by Jen Bair

One Good Eye

<u>Huntress and Harvester series</u> by Jessica Raney

A Seed Once Sown

<u>Wrong Way series</u> by Kevin Pettway

Wrong Way to Heaven

<u>Invasion of the Chromium</u> by William LJ Galaini

Chromium Rise

<u>Pick's Pocket</u> by C.M. McGuire

Beer For My Corpses

<u>The Kin</u> by Ethan A. Cooper

All Hail the Kin

Gullhome
Oldam's Tempest
Norrik
Icebite
Spiny Oyster River
Raiders Sea
Summervatn
Vikkan
Krysuvik
Badiron
Disn
Maiten
The
Tyrran
Knarrax
Summer Trades
Mirrik
Gradeep
Pyjin
Brinland River
Green
Sinad
Low
Wood
Rousea
Wolf Tusk
Rousland
Dalmi
The Arlean
Arlea
Sleed
Sejent
Sedrios
Whipse
Southlen
N
W
E
S
The Paradisals
Dingid
Runfish
Port Placid
Wolf
Lan

Full-color map at KevinPettway.com

To every motherfucker just trying to get by.

CHAPTER
ONE

A person only ventured into the Rottering swamp of Sedrios if they absolutely had to. That or they just had terrible standards. The stink of the water seeped into the air and beat travelers down like a thug looking for money. Half the fish in the waters weren't edible.

It was also the home of Pickett, bona fide swamp witch and proprietress of the Pick's Pocket—the only bar as far as the stinking waters spread.

The Pick's Pocket was, perhaps, the most profitable bar in the swamp. This was due to its untarnishable reputation for being the only bar in the swamp. And, being the only bar in the swamp, it didn't have to be charming or cozy. It simply needed alcohol, entertainment, and a temporary shelter from the stink. Anyone who ventured far enough into the swamp to reach it knew the one unbreachable rule: don't risk the wrath of the swamp witch.

So why? Why, in spite of her carefully crafted reputation, did Pickett still have to deal with the likes of sleaze-balls and demi-divas?

"What do you mean when you say 'weak constitution?'"

snarled Pickett, her thick frizz of dark stormy hair prickling with her growing rage. "Romona's performed here four times already to substantial tips. What about my establishment suddenly fails to meet her highness's esteemed standards?"

Pickett threw back the edge of her colorful, star-patterned cape just enough to show off her belt and the glittering bottles that hung from it, each one promising a different horrible fate.

Romona's manager took a step back, grimacing as the floor-board creaked and sagged under his heel. His already pale face paled further as he smoothed his waistcoat and raised his round, trembling chin. "She heard rumors. Stories about . . . about unsavory things happening out here to women of her standing and reputation."

Pickett scowled. Oh she knew. The latest juicy story to bounce around among the traders and fishermen was one in which a noblewoman ignorant of the importance of incognito travel had foolishly opted to ride her horse along the stretches of wooden walkways erected across miles of swamp. As the story went, the woman, deprived of her fine perfumes, was so overcome by the stink of swamp water that she fell off her horse and right into the muck. She'd woken, half drowned but still clinging to life, dragged to the safety of the walkway by a hero who'd made off with everything but her undergarments.

Pickett never should have allowed Romona to sit and talk to any of those idiots. "Surely she's smart enough not to travel the boardwalks dripping in jewels. And smart enough not to break a contract with a witch."

The manager let out a small squeak and glanced around, but nothing and nobody would be there to help him. Yet somehow, he mustered whatever passed for courage and carried on. "You must understand, Romona Ovlovey's unique talents necessitate a careful and consistent environment of—"

"You mean she caught the eye of some rich prick and decided she was too good to keep up her contract with miserable . . ."

She leaned forward onto the wooden table, grasping its rough edge with one hand. "Old . . ." Well, she was in her twenties so that didn't really track, but it felt like the word to use as she grabbed the table with her other hand, half pulling herself over it. "*Witchy* Pickett of the Rottering swamp?"

Sharp bursts of light flashed at the edges of the bar, like the dancing light on the Sedrios swamps but focused. Dangerous. Threatening.

The manager didn't step back again, but his hand plunged into his pocket. If Pickett knew him properly, it was probably so he could clutch an effigy of the old god Oldam. Funny. He didn't look like a man of Greenshade. Probably someone clamoring to any force he thought might listen and prove to be more powerful than her. Best of luck to him, really. An old slab of rocks was hardly going to come to his aid.

"Romona owes me eight more shows." She growled. "I made this newfound career of hers possible in the first place, remember?"

"You gave her a stage to sing on," he said, albeit with a trembling voice. "She's the one who got traders talking. She's the one who attracted a more—"

"Say it." Pickett snarled, and the lights flashed bright enough to look, for a moment, like lightning.

The manager took a deep breath. "The venue she's committed to is more appropriate for her current status. A status she *earned*."

Thunder clapped through the small space of the bar. An acrid smell filled the air. The manager yelped, his trousers darkening right around the crotch, before he turned and fled.

Pickett sighed and dragged a rickety chair from one of the tables and flopped dramatically down into it, her star-embroidered cape fluttering around her. Maybe she should have a bigger one made. One that could really express her irritation with the world. But Edie had done the best she could with the materials she'd had on hand.

"I'm gonna have to clean up his piss, now," she muttered.

"Sorry, Pickett," Edie called. There was a clanging of pans before a young woman stepped out, her straw-blonde hair gathered in a messy bun atop her head. She held out a mug of beer in one hand and smiled weakly.

Pickett glowered but took it all the same, downing half the drink in one pull. She burped softly, smeared the foam from her upper lip, and sighed. "Nah, Edie. It's not your fault."

"I don't know. I think, if I'd stopped to think, I could have done better thunder and lightning was all I could think of on short notice." Edie perched on top of the table in front of Pickett, tapping her ankles together under her rosy skirt. "I tried to time the effects to the conversation, but it looks like I didn't scare him quite enough. Maybe I should have tried the ghost trick."

"The ghost trick's not ready. Besides, I doubt anything would be enough to drag Romona back. It sounds like she's moved on to finer things." Pickett held up her mug and sneered. "To turncoats who don't care if they leave a poor old swamp witch in the cold!"

Edie arched a brow. "Well, I mean, maybe if you were a real swamp witch."

"And who but you knows that?" Pickett stared down into the mug for a moment before a wicked smile curled at the corners of her lips. "At least if she believes it, she might just think that every misfortune for the rest of her life is a lingering curse from the swamp witch. My revenge will simmer without my even having to light the fire."

"A very happy parting gift indeed," Edie said dryly. "But that does leave us with a bit of a problem. If you want to sell drinks to traders, you need to give them a reason to stay once they've finished their business. We both know the drink here isn't good enough on its own."

Pickett snorted and knocked back the rest of her mug before dropping it on the floor, spraying bits of bitter Sedrian beer onto the floor with the little puddle of manager piss.

It was true, of course. There wasn't much point in buying anything expensive to sell in a run-down shack of a place like the Pick's Pocket. Since the whole building was a shamble of boards held together by ropes and prayers, the cost of repairs ate up any excess they might have earned by having a firm hold on the swamp market. At least the Rottering one. And it was those same costs that might eventually shut her doors for good. Every broken floorboard, every hole in the wall was more coin she couldn't throw at the debt of I initial buy, and Sedrian moneylenders weren't known for their generosity. Nor were her regulars known for their deep pockets.

Romona had been an actual draw, someone to convince the fishermen to come more frequently, someone to convince the traders to stay longer and spend more. Without entertainment, who was going to buy a third drink, much less a fourth or a fifth? Pickett could always perform "magic" but that could be risky. Too much magic exposure and sooner or later some keen eye would catch that she was a fake, and any protection she had from brigands, marauders, and general dickheads would evaporate.

No. She needed her reputation, and she needed money fast. If the rent and repairs were neglected for too long, the whole bar would collapse into the swamp, and her moneylender would have her head.

"Don't suppose you can sing?" Pickett asked.

Edie laughed and hopped off the table. "Sure. I used to sing. Back when I was a milkmaid I'd sing to the cows while I worked. I think they moo'd just to cover the sound of it."

"Useless," Pickett muttered. "Why do I keep you around?"

"Because even swamp witches get lonely." Edie patted Pickett's shoulder. "And someone's got to make a little food to feed your patrons."

Despite her dour mood, Pickett patted Edie's hand right back. It was hard not to give in to that excessive cheer. It was like her own personal sunbeam whenever she wanted it.

"Yeah, well. I haven't got more entertainment coming for a fortnight and we're hand-to-mouth as is. If I can't sort this out, you may need to seek new employment."

"I'm sure the cows will take me back." Edie smiled and straightened. "Now, I think the rum boy'll be here soon. I'll go make room in the supply cupboard."

"He may need to find new employment too," she huffed. "Somewhere else to take his silly shanties."

As Edie headed back into the kitchen to get some actual work done, Pickett closed her eyes and allowed herself a solid minute of wallowing. She still had to clean the floors and get ready for travelers in the afternoon. That left her with only a couple of hours to come up with a solution. She was just lucky Edie had come along and was personable enough to handle liquor deliveries.

Pickett opened her eyes. Liquor deliveries. Like the rum boy.

The rum boy! The rum boy with his silly shanties!

"Edie!" she shouted. "Get a mop and clean up in here. I'll handle the rum boy."

Edie popped her head out of the kitchen, frowning deeply.

"You hate the rum boy. You call him pedantic."

"Yes. Even so." Pickett flourished her rune-embroidered cape with almost all the drama the situation warranted. "Tonight, the rum boy will become a profitable rum man!"

CHAPTER

TWO

Pickett didn't give the kid a chance. As soon as the rum boy dropped off the shipment, she dragged him into the back room and shoved a coin in his hand. She told him in no uncertain terms, "You're going to sing for us tonight."

To which he looked ready to vomit.

Kellum was about as typical a Sedrios boy as anyone could hope to meet. As far as Pickett was concerned, it wasn't necessarily a good thing. He came from a small town and carried many of those old superstitions around with him. The ones that told of drowned children, fog, and swamp witches. Good for building a local folklore Pickett profited from. Bad for all the people who grew up in those towns deprived of the rich soil of life that might allow them to sprout interesting personalities. Most of them were about as thrilling as the barley they grew, and they didn't even have the world experience to know how dull they were.

Perhaps the cleverest thing Kellum had ever done in his life was march out of his muddy little village and get a job transporting rum from merchant traders on the coast to whoever would buy from him. Nine days out of ten, that was the only use

Pickett had for him. He could keep his sweet opinions about wild things that lived in the trees and his observations about what a right and friendly person this or that drunk was. She got enough of the village talk from her patrons. So long as he brought his wares, it was more than enough company for her.

This was the one day out of the ten that he would prove himself to be more than a booze peddler. So as soon as he'd dropped off the bottles, Pickett shut the door and pushed the empty bottle boxes in front of it. Not a strong barricade for a big guy like Kellum, but it was something.

Kellum turned and blinked at the bottles, then cocked his head to the side.

"Um, Miss Pickett, the bottles have to go in the cart."

"Not yet they don't." Pickett grinned and drummed her fingers on the door. "You're not going anywhere. Not yet."

"Oh." Kellum glanced left then right, as he nibbled on his thumbnail. "When can I go?"

"Not until after nightfall."

His eyes widened, and he turned red as a bloodberry. "Oh, Miss Pickett, um, see the thing is I respect you a lot but I never had the notion . . . You're awfully pretty and all but—"

Oh shit. Pickett cleared her throat. "Not like that. I need you to perform."

"Perform?" The red didn't leave his cheeks. "Oh, that's very kind of you, but I'm no performer. I'm just dropping off the rum."

Pickett shrugged. "You sing. My stage is empty. Let's make this work."

"I'd rather not."

Pickett narrowed her eyes. "Are you going to turn this into a fight?"

"Um." Kellum glanced over his shoulder, as if someone might magically appear to get him out of this, then grimaced. "Maybe?"

So that's how it was going to be. "Kellum, my evening crowd will be here in three hours. That's three hours you have to keep pissing me off and fighting me until I turn you into a worm, or it's three hours you have to rehearse."

"I guess I pick not a worm?"

Pickett nodded sagely. "Good choice."

She set Kellum up in the kitchen to practice his singing, which irritated her less now that it was going to earn her a bit of coin. Pickett unloaded the rum, checked that their beer was still good, sort of vaguely swept a broom about as though it was possible to keep the place clean, and tried to keep a positive outlook on the evening.

The customers started shuffling in, mostly fishermen looking to toast or curse the day's work or merchants looking to trade. Time for the show.

Why Pickett actually thought this would go as smoothly as she hoped, she had no idea. But there was Kellum sitting in the corner, his knees pulled up to his chest and his fingers laced together behind his head.

Pickett scowled.

"Kellum, I thought we established that I would turn you into a worm if you refused to perform."

"I-I-I can't. I'm no singer! A few shanties while I work isn't the same as an audience." He lifted his head to reveal red-rimmed eyes and a nose that was definitely dripping.

Ugh. If this was what it was like to be a manager, no wonder Romona's was such a mess.

"Look," Pickett snapped, "all you have to do is go up there, sing some of those songs you picked up from the coast, and you get half of whatever's in the basket. Come on."

Pickett grabbed Kellum's wrists and hauled him to his feet. She circled him once, then twice for good measure. "Look. You can go out there and caterwaul like a kitten. But if you have a good look, people will tolerate you."

He rubbed his nose on his sleeve, leaving behind a snotty trail. "Is that why you're never scared? Because of that fancy cape Miss Edie made you?"

"Yeah. Sure. Clothes can be our armor, right? Now let me have a look at you."

His hair was messy, but in a roguish sort of way when she ruffled it. His clothing wasn't anything special, but unbuttoning the collar and wrapping a cloth around his neck made him a little more flashy. Not Romona Ovlovey flashy and certainly nowhere near Pickett's own fashion, but it was better. Besides, as long as he turned around enough to give the audience a glimpse of that very taut backside, they'd get all the show they needed. She grinned and clapped him on the shoulder. "You're always singing anyway. Might as well let me pay you for it."

"Yes. But . . . You see, I'm only singing to myself." Kellum shifted from one foot to the other, then yelped as the wood under his foot bowed and cracked, filling the air with the scent of fresh rot.

Damn. Pickett should have repaired that board the last time she had any money in her pocket to do so.

"You see?" She gestured at the floor. "I could use the money. You could use the money. Money is good. So go earn us some."

Kellum stared down at her, his bright blue eyes wide with fear. "I've never done it on a stage before. In front of people. I'm sure these folks'd be much happier to see Ms. Ovlovey."

"Fuck Ms. Ovlovey," Pickett hissed. "Ms. Ovlovey picked brighter stages than this one and you know what the Pick's Pocket means to every trader and traveler in this stinking swamp. And also you don't want to be turned into a worm."

Kellum ducked his head. "But, well, still. I've never done it in front of a crowd before. I feel like simple old Kellum's not enough for a whole audience. Maybe you should just-just hex me and get it over with, miss."

Pickett couldn't stop the roll of her eyes. She should've been running the bar. Edie was the one capable of batting her eyes and winning over a simple creature like Kellum. Bless her, maybe it was easier to make friends because Edie actually believed all the kind things she had to say about people.

Of course, when Pickett glanced up at Kellum, he'd gone two shades paler and very nearly wet himself like Ovlovey's manager. What had she been thinking?

Pickett pasted on a sickly smile. "Let me just . . . I'm going to handle some of that fine rum you've brought for us. You just sit still. See if you can remember any of your songs. Your fiddle's in the cart, right?"

"I play the mandolin."

"Same difference."

The Pick's Pocket was well and truly fucked six ways to the end of the fucking world.

Pickett slipped behind the bar, reaching automatically for one of the bottles Kellum had brought. They didn't have their most exceptional crowds that night: a couple of merchants, one of whom had a tag-along, another pair could have been anyone from anywhere, a couple of mercenaries, travelers, anything, really, some probable farmers or hunters, and someone with a baby goat with a rough rope looped around its neck. The kid paced, antsy and bored, and occasionally turned and sprinted toward the table, smacking its head into one of the legs and causing the beers to spill. One of these days Pickett was going to get good at enforcing the "No Animals" policy, but this was not the night for it. She needed every tiny bronze shim she could wring out of them. The last thing she needed to do was put them off by denying them their . . . What? Pets? Trade? Dinner? One never knew what someone intended to do with a goat.

Edie glanced up and arched a brow. "Well? Is he ready?"

"Like a tomcat in a swimming race. You'd better go talk him out of his head. I don't want to clean up the sick if he upchucks all the butterflies in his belly."

Edie rolled her eyes and gave Pickett's shoulder a gentle swat. "Be nice. But I'll talk to him. Northfellow's asked for his usual."

"Oh, so he wants the good old days and the warriors he used to fight alongside." Pickett slumped onto the bar. "Let me just see if we've got any of that in a barrel in the back."

"Be nice. He's a harmless old fellow."

"I'm always nice. Couldn't find a nicer swamp witch."

"That's not saying much."

Pickett rolled her eyes. "If being nice paid, then paupers would dine on cake and moneylenders would starve."

"If you say so."

Edie smiled indulgently, and Pickett watched her go, a tightness in her chest that was at once familiar and unfamiliar.

"How'd you get a pretty young thing like that to chain herself to this miserable dump?" Arn, a fisherman with a hairy mole on his upper lip asked as he, too, watched Edie depart. "How does a proprietress with your sour attitude lure in a stray like that?"

"Sour attitude? I'll have you know I'm sweet as honey. That's how you lure in good help."

Arn snorted into his drink. It just proved one thing Pickett had known for a long time. The truth was often harder to believe.

"I could enchant her given half the chance," he mumbled.

Pickett shot him a glare. "Try it and I'll feed you to the swamp beast, Arn."

Arn snorted. "Ain't a real thing, and you know it."

Pickett honestly didn't know one way or another, but she wasn't about to go hunting the waters for a giant, man-eating monster. Best to let it live in legend the same way she did.

At least, the way she had until now, until she couldn't anymore.

As she dumped a hefty slug of bibblewood juice into a glass, she considered raising it to toast the death of the Pick's Pocket. Romona Ovlovey had abandoned her. Kellum didn't have the stones to stomp out onto that stage. Either she learned to turn her swamp witch story into a real show or most of these merchants and traders would decide it wasn't worth the trouble of staying too long at a place like this. And what would happen to her? What would happen to Edie?

Pickett set the glass back down on the wood of the bar that needed a fresh coat of wax. Maybe better for things to fall apart when the place was on the verge of doing the same. She poured a generous portion of rum atop the juice and slid the glass across the bar toward the Northfellow. He grunted, blinking so violently that his thick, wiry white brows shook like swamp grass in the wind, then took his rum and juice and sipped appreciatively before hunching over it like he was a cat with a dead mouse.

Nobody much knew his name. The few times he'd said something that could have been his name, it had been something strange and difficult to pronounce, and Pickett vaguely felt as though she was insulting him when she tried and failed. So he was, had always been, and would always be, the Northfellow.

And what would happen to him? He practically lived on that stool at the corner of the bar, smelling like fish and fermenting body odor. He'd be just as hopelessly lost as Pickett and Edie and the handful of other regulars who had to wander out along the rickety wooden walkways of the swamp in order to find a place to drink and not hate the whole world for a few hours.

The Northfellow clutched the glass close. Close enough that she worried he'd squeeze it enough to crack it. He'd better not. She only had actual glassware to serve because a trader had gotten horribly drunk, nearly bankrupted himself buying rounds for everyone and accidentally exposing himself. A dozen real glass pieces had been what he'd been able to use to at least pay the debt off to her. She hadn't seen him since. Probably because he'd exposed himself to a local meja's secretary and that'd come back to bite him. Generally, crossing the leader of a town was a bad idea. Even Pickett knew that.

Pickett prepared a few more drinks, dropping them off at the tables. Coins were dropped. Beer and rum were spilled. The baby goat nibbled at her boot before she shook it off with a scowl and shooed it back to its distracted owner.

"Well, if our business is done for the night, I'd best be going." A merchant grunted, pushing himself up from his seat.

One of his companions gestured toward the stage. "You don't want to wait for the entertainment?"

"What entertainment? Good night, lads."

And just like that, he and all the coins in his pocket headed for the door. Fuck Romona north and south. Without entertainment, her customers had no reason to stay longer than their business. More than that, they had no reason to keep spending their money. Frantically, Pickett tried to work out some way to force him to stay. Some new sort of drink, perhaps? The offer of a round for his table if they all stayed and paid for another?

Before she could cast out a desperate offer, a figure stepped out from the back, skirts swirling around their ankles as they spun onto the stage.

Pickett blinked. Black fabric with bits of gray lace twirled into flowers along the hem. That was one of Romona's dresses. Had she been so eager to take her new job that she'd left a dress behind? Not that Pickett had time to mill over it as the figure spun around, black skirts flaring like a dark blossom.

A polite applause rose among those patrons who remained, but it was replaced with gasps and scandalized whispers as Kellum spun around. He wore Romona's dress, Romona's hat, even a touch of rouge on his cheeks. The nervous rum boy was gone and in his place was a star.

The merchant at the door paused, then wandered back to the bar. His gaze was fixed on the man on the stage. Pickett grinned and slid him a glass of bibblewood juice and rum. Without glancing over at her, he dropped a couple of shims onto the bar and drank. Pickett had no idea what Edie had said to Kellum. As she poured another drink and added more coin to her till, she didn't care.

Kellum threw his arms into the air, lifted his chin, and opened his mouth. And there it was. That voice. That beautiful voice that grated so often on Pickett's ears latched onto each and every patron like a hook. So much so they might as well not have heard the dreadful lyrics, a typical port song he must have picked up from one of his rum merchants.

> "She told me she had never known
> A lover in her past.
> Yet as she raised her skirts I saw
> A red and angry rash."

Great guffaws of laughter rose up. That magnificent, stupid rum boy. Had Pickett ever said an unkind thing about him? Surely not. He was nothing short of a sensation as he danced from one end of the stage to another.

The patrons of the Pick's Pocket began to clap along, laughing and cheering as Kellum swirled, even shaking his hips as he sang another verse.

> "I knew I ought to hesitate
> And yet he coaxed me in.
> But as I rolled his breeches down
> I knew I'd never win!"

Another round was called. Then another. One table after another, all of them cheering and laughing as Kellum, in Romona's dress, won more laughs than any before. Edie laughed, skipping back behind the bar, her pale face flushed.

"Isn't he incredible?" She laughed, seizing Pickett's hand and giving it a tug. Edie's fingers were deceptively rough and strong, the only thing about her that didn't give the appearance of being soft and gentle. If she wanted, she could easily drag Pickett out. But she didn't.

Pickett huffed and nodded. "How'd you get him on the stage?"

Edie batted her eyes. "A girl has her secrets. And the dress was his idea. He said it was easier to do this if he wasn't doing it as Kellum."

"Oh?" Pickett arched a brow. "Then if that's not Kellum, who's up there performing?"

"To be decided later." Edie squeezed Pickett's hands. "Come on. Let's have a dance."

Pickett pulled her hand back. "You're the dancer. You have your fun. Someone's got to keep the Northfellow in his drinks."

The Northfellow, however, gazed at the patched-wood wall, his eyes glassy and his white, scraggly beard dipping into his drink.

Edie pulled a face and pulled at the edge of Pickett's patch-work cape.

"He can keep for a song. Even you, Pickett, need to let yourself have a little fun. Dancing is good for the soul."

Was it? It was an awfully charming thing to believe. And Edie had one of those guileless smiles. The sort that could grab a person and drag them down, down, down into a pool of joy. Edie was the sort of person the world loved to hurt.

"I danced with someone once." Pickett sniffed, crossing her arms. "It wasn't for me. But you go. Watching you enjoy yourself gives me enough pleasure."

Edie stared for a long moment, but she didn't reach for Pickett again. "Well, I'll see about what tips I can muster," she said, pulling the woven basket out from under the bar. And then, she danced from table to table, winking and twirling her skirts. Bronze shims and copper pips found their way into her basket and, on one occasion, Pickett could swear she saw Arn's plump friend Slurne toss in a silver scale before reaching out, trying to touch Edie's bottom. But Edie twirled out of the way just in time, smacking the back of his head with the heavier-than-usual basket.

Kellum gave a proud stomp as he leaned over, winking at the goat's owner.

> "An innocent no longer can
> I honest claim to be.
> Yet every sailor thinks he's got
> My sweet virginity!"

The crowds roared with laughter. Kellum twirled and sank into a deep bow before reaching for his mandolin to start another. Edie returned to the bar, dropping the basket in front of her. It clanged just a bit louder than it had in the past.

Perhaps, impossible as it seemed, Romona had helped them by abandoning the bar. Pickett grinned and poured a slug of rum for herself, for Edie, and for her new main act.

THREE

Pickett leaned back in her creaky, vine-woven chair and stared out at the brown waters of the Rottering swamp. Dawn was just a few hours away, now, but that didn't stop all manner of wildlife from caterwauling enough to wake the dead. But that was as peaceful as it got out here. The breeze played with the outermost layer of frizz in her hair, not unlike the gentle touch of someone about to twist and weave it into something beautiful, and the feel of it always put her at ease.

The fact that their last traveler had just left made it a long, good night. She waved lazily as half a dozen of her customers tottered cheerfully across the wooden walkways, their trading done for the night and their bellies full of booze. Kellum was among them, pulling his now-empty cart behind him with a new spring in his step. Even from this distance, she could almost hear the jingle in his pouch from his take of the tips.

What a glorious evening. Romona may have been a hell of a singer, but Kellum was the one the merchants would make a detour to come and see the next time the rum boy was able to take a night to perform. Romona would never have sung a song about crotch crickets and genital warts.

But how long would it last? Nobody liked having to delve into the swamp to get from one place to another. She caught the business of those who did, but the rumor was that there would soon be a new road built along one of the borders of the swamp. A new, safer, less-smelly means of travel. Which meant whatever power in Sedrios was in charge of occasionally coming in to maintaining these boardwalks had a road to worry about. What would they care about commerce in this swamp? Pick's Pocket would be dead in the dirty water.

Pickett took a sip of Kellum's rum from her wooden cup; all the glass ones had been used during the festivities. As rum, it fell into the category of good enough. It burned like fire piss and left a funny aftertaste, but nobody had been poisoned yet. It was nice to dream of someday being able to afford nicer stuff. For the moment, the travelers of the swamp were lucky Pickett could afford even this stuff.

Of course, that was getting ahead of herself. Nicer product and better conditions were something she could buy only once she no longer had to pay month by month to keep the old shack in her name, to keep patching the holes and leaks of old and rotting wood, to keep putting off the fear of losing the only home she'd ever had control over, along with the other consequences of failing to repay a debt.

Kellum's performance had helped. More than that. He'd been incredible. But he was still the rum boy. Shipments came only every other week, and only if weather and other unhelpful conditions allowed it. Even if he could become a regular, one performance every fortnight wasn't going to make the coin she needed. Romona had been scheduled to sing twice weekly. A quarter of the appearances for Kellum might just mean he'd gain a reputation with all the speed of a squid in soil. She needed a new act, something reliable night after night to keep the patrons around and spending their coin, something that would be a big enough draw even if a new road offered her patrons other alternatives. Maybe she could find an act big enough to earn her money to maintain some of these boardwalks on her own and ensure all traffic had to swing by the Pick's Pocket.

She sniffed at her rum again and frowned. Being the only bar in the Rottering swamp was only as good as the traffic. Gods knew she didn't buy nice enough liquor. The Pick's Pocket was a dump. But it was her dump. She'd built it up herself, she'd poured everything she had into it. And, for the first time in her life, she had something big and it was hers.

"Pickett?" The door creaked open as Edie poked her head out. "I'm heading to bed. Are you ready to take this shift?"

Pickett smirked a little to herself. Well, hers and the stray the gods had seen fit to send her.

"Funds counted?" she asked.

"And spills and dishes cleaned," Edie said, crossing her arms. "You, my devious friend, are now two scales and a few shims richer with a clean bar to boot."

"A nice clean-up of a shit situation." Pickett mused. "Lucky you got the rum boy to perform. Now we just need to stay afloat until our next shipment."

Edie arched a brow. "After such an exciting night, you're honestly able to stay up at all longer? How did you ever keep this place running without someone to share the watch with you?"

"I used to sleep a lot less." Pickett spared her a smile, then set her cup aside, tugging out her pipe. There ought to be enough punch to her shag to keep her awake for the next few hours, at least until it was Edie's turn to take watch.

As Pickett tucked the end of the pipe between her lips, Edie squeezed her shoulder.

"You could always borrow a book, you know. It's so dull just keeping an eye open this late."

"And miss all this excitement?" She gestured at the swamp grasses rustling in the breeze.

Edie crossed her arms and looked Pickett up and down, her pretty face pinched but not tense.

"It's not because you lied about being able to read, is it?"

Pickett snorted, though it was a fair enough accusation. "I don't lie to you, Edie. You know that."

"I do. I just wish I knew what was going on in that head of yours, sometimes. I've told you everything about me, Pickett. Everything. And you . . ."

Yes. She knew. She would take Edie's past deeds to the grave, and Edie? Well, she didn't need to know Pickett's past deeds. Pickett glanced up. "I tell you what I want you to know and what's a concern. The rest is junk."

"I know. Still, I wish." Edie rapped Pickett's head gently with her knuckles, and then she was gone, the door shutting behind her.

Why the gods had seen fit to fling such a charming creature into the swamp, Pickett still couldn't quite grasp. But she wasn't going to complain. The second Edie had barged through that door, she'd managed to knock down Pickett's walls and end up in the rare, tender bit of her heart still capable of letting someone in. Of course afterwards Edie'd killed a man and Pickett had to help her dump the body, but still. It was nice to have a friend. If the gods chose to favor her with good company, she'd accept it. So long as they didn't mind her going about her ever-so-disreputable business with a little less loneliness than before, she would take it.

Pickett leaned back in her chair, content to puff away on her pipe. A bit over two scales. She owed two just for the month. And that was before the cost of food, drink, and the endless incidentals of keeping a place running in the swamp. Hell, the bar itself couldn't be worth much more than three. But this was good. This was almost enough to keep her going a little longer. Eventually, she'd scrape together enough to pay the debt on this place, stop pissing away interest, and actually start turning some profit.

As thick plumes of smoke rose up to the sky, the moonlight danced on the swamp water. And something stirred below the surface.

Pickett furrowed her brows, leaning forward without bothering to slip the wooden lip of the pipe out from between her lips. Swamps could be strange, especially this close to ship channels. But even so, there was seldom anything active enough to stir the surface of the water this close to the noise and calamity of a bar. Even with the occasional scrap of food tossed out in the water, it wasn't like Pickett to serve anything that a water predator might find appealing.

She nibbled on the bit of her pipe for a moment before leaning forward, peering into the dark water. Something shifted again, sending ripples up to the surface. Then, like it had been launched from a sling, something slimy and silver about the size of her hand flew up from the water. Pickett leaped from her seat, prepared to kick it off the boardwalk, but she froze.

It was a fish.

But it wasn't just a fish.

It flopped, around, fins flapping, mouth snapping as a hazy, glassy eye rolled back in its head, then forward.

Pickett knelt down, tapping the pipe against her chin. Despite the fish's energetic flipping, it had serious wounds. A huge chunk had been ripped from its head. Another had been taken from its stomach, enough for her to make out its guts that had gone dull, like they'd been pulled from its body and left out for a week. Yet still, the creature wriggled and moved. It should have been dead. So why wasn't it?

An idea itched in the back of her mind, growing until it scratched like a claw into her brain. What better way to perpetuate her reputation as a sorcerer than as a woman who'd reached across the veil and brought life back to something that absolutely should not survive? How much might an already drunk patron pay for a glimpse? Perhaps enough coin to get on top of her debt before it swallowed her.

With a grin, Pickett dipped around the back of the building into the shed before returning, bucket in hand. The thing continued to writhe and struggle. It seemed not even its time in the air was enough to slow it down.

"How would you like to earn a little bit of fame, you wee bugger?" she whispered, scooping up a generous tug of swamp water before she nudged the fish in with her foot. It'd be another fortnight before Kellum performed again, but that didn't mean Pickett would have to go without.

EDIE CROSSED HER ARMS, glaring down at the little bucket between them. She still had the red of sleep in her eyes, but there wasn't time for her to brew something to wake her up. The sun was high, the day was young, and the possibilities were bright.

"A fish?" Edie grumbled.

"Not just a fish. Dream a little!" Pickett clasped the sides of the bucket and leaned forward, eyes wide. "It's a dead fish that swims. It flip flops and moves. It could give people a glimpse of life after death. Think of what a show it is!"

"Yes. Quite the show." Edie arched a brow. "Pickett, this isn't a good thing."

"Sure it is. We can charge people to have a look at something they've never seen before."

Edie planted one hand on her hip and gestured sharply at the bucket with the other. "Pickett, it's dead and it's moving. It's proof the swamp is cursed. Or poisoned."

Pickett waved it off. "Strange things happen. You've heard the stories about the wailing fog."

"Stories and the real thing are different."

"Oh come on. Some actual demon or idiot with a magic object might've dumped something in the swamp. I'm sure it's already spread out too thin to do any damage." Pickett pointed at the bucket. "If it was really dangerous, I'm sure we'd be seeing worse than a moving dead fish."

"Or this could be the start of something very bad."

Edie was sensitive about that sort of thing, and offending Edie in this moment would only build a headache that would benefit nobody.

"Well, my dear kitchen girl, it's here whether you like it or not. And think of what people would pay to duck into the back room to have a glimpse at life beyond certain death?"

"And which room will I be clearing out?" Edie scoffed. "Better that I just hang curtains around the stage and act as a gatekeeper charging customers to stick their heads inside."

"If that's what it takes."

Edie shook her head. "This itches me wrong, Pickett." She took a step back, wrapping her hands around her waist. "Dead things in the swamp moving around. It's not natural. Doesn't feel like something we should fool with."

A fresh scoff was right on the tip of Pickett's tongue when it finally clicked. Edie was sinking into herself, annoyance slipping all too quickly into something very, very wrong. Edie was meant for smiling and dancing. And Pickett, clearly, was meant for dumbassery.

"I . . ." she had to dig through her brain to find something to say that wasn't acerbic or sarcastic. "I mean, I was sitting right outside. If anything, you know, *bigger* was going to come up, I'd have seen it."

Edie just clenched her jaw. "I don't like this, Pickett."

"Hey." Pickett took a step toward her, looking Edie up and down, working out what she ought to do next. Hug her? Pat her head? Pour her a drink? Edie might as well have been a different species.

She settled for resting a hand on Edie's shoulder. Edie didn't respond. Not a good sign.

"I don't think it's . . . I mean . . ." Pickett sighed. She knew Edie was afraid the body they'd dumbed in the swamp might come back just like this fish had. "It's not Marnoc. We took care of him. It's just a fish."

"For now," Edie muttered.

"If I see any sign that there's anything dangerous going on, I'll figure it out. I'll keep us safe." Not that she was about to let herself believe something was going to happen. Marnoc had been dead for months. There couldn't be anything left of him.

Edie nodded stiffly. "Yeah. I hope you're right. Maybe we'd be better off finding a new act. An actual person we can rely upon more than once in a while."

"Right, because acts are swarming to perform at a waystation in the muck." Pickett drew back and gestured broadly. "However will we sort through all the musicians and escapologists and family circuses clamoring to show off their vast skills for us, hm?"

Edie ducked her chin, glaring at the floor before she tucked a strand of hair behind her ear. Despite her fiery gaze, her lip gave a small twitch that made something warm pool in Pickett's stomach. There was that smile, just trying to claw its way back out.

"You could always do tricks." Edie suggested in a small voice.

"You mean like the fog from the ceiling or the flash bangs from my cape pockets?" Pickett scowled, gripping her lapels. "Those tricks are limited. And if people catch on that I can only do them one at a time, they'll figure it out. How do you think the kind of vagabonds who come in here will act as soon as they realize the swamp witch hasn't got any more magic than a toad?"

"You're giving them too much credit," Edie mumbled, but the smile settled back on her lips, small but undeniably there. "You could always try reciting crude poetry. *'There once was a widow from Greenshade—'*"

A knock at the door sent them both jumping. Edie grabbed a towel from the bar and tossed it over the top of the bucket. Pickett, meanwhile, peered through the crack between the slats. At first, she saw nothing but the slow-rotting planks of the board-walk and the gray, brackish waters of the swamp. Shifting her gaze downward, she saw the top of a head swamped with dark curls. And probably lice. She couldn't confirm it, but she'd guess there were lice.

Before swinging open the door, Pickett nodded back at Edie, who relaxed just a little. The curly-haired boy tromped through the entrance, somehow managing to track in a fresh coat of dirt that stood out amidst the dirt that had already taken up resi-dence inside. He sniffed, wiping his nose on a grimy sleeve before he dug through the many pockets of his patched jacket and pulled out a folded letter.

"Afternoon, miss," he said with a little shrug. "You know the deal."

Yes, Pickett knew the deal all too well. If she was honest with herself, she'd have been happy to take him in the same way she had Edie. Except Edie was grown and knew how to clean up after herself, and adolescent boys ate enough to put Pickett out of business within a week. There was something about that age. She remembered eating that much when she was young, so it was hard to resent those who'd turned her away.

"Edie?" She glanced over her shoulder. "Mind fetching a shim for the sharkbait?"

"Already on it," Edie announced, as she tossed a coin at Pickett.

Pickett caught it easily and set it in the upturned palm of the messenger. "All right, Letterboy. Give it."

Letterboy dropped the letter into her palm before biting the coin then pocketing it. If he was at all curious about the missives he delivered, that curiosity dissolved the second he had another coin in hand. He glanced around, then turned, eyes widening. "What's that?" he asked, pointing at the covered bucket.

Pickett didn't bother answering, because, even before he finished asking, Letterboy wove around her and tugged the towel off. He was something of a stray cat, tame when it suited him but prone to do whatever he wanted. Yeah, Pickett knew the type all too well. As long as he didn't cause trouble or nick anything, Pickett didn't much care what he did.

She broke the seal and unfolded the page. She had only to see the loopy, oversized signature at the bottom of the letter and, just like that, her stomach knotted itself into something even the cleverest sailor couldn't unwind.

She forced her face into the stinking expression of irritation, if only to hide the fear from Letterboy. But she couldn't stop herself from glancing around at her bar, with its mismatched chairs, its rotting boards, and its chipped and shoddy drinkware. All of it, down to the last rusty nail, belonged to her, just as much as it belonged to someone else.

A bit over two years ago, Pickett had discovered an old fisherman's shack, falling apart and ready to decay into the swamp. The man had given it to her for a song. He was old. He was tired. And the pervading chill and stink of the swamp through deteriorating walls had finally forced him to bury his pride and move in with his daughter's family by the coast.

At the time, it seemed like a perfect purchase. Cheap enough for her meager savings and a near certainty that she alone could attract the traders, merchants, and fishermen that wandered the boardwalks day and night. She'd thought she was so terribly clever.

But Pickett, as she soon realized, was about as clever as she was a sorcerer.

It was one thing to purchase an inexpensive property. It was another thing to make it livable. And it was a near disaster to afford everything it took to turn it into a proper business. But every rotting board and rusting nail was hers. All hers. It wasn't something she knew how to express to just anyone, in part because "anyone" consisted mostly of rot-wads. But there was something to be said for belonging. Not just being beholden to family or the "family" that bought someone when the other family fucked off to wherever. This was hers. If she shared a room, it's because she let a certain kitchen maid share it in return for her work. If the planks were rotten, they were hers to manage. If a patron was rude, she could boot him into the swamp. Pickett had never had so much freedom and control since she'd first sucked in the breath of this greedy world. She couldn't give up once she finally had something of her own.

Except for the tiny bit where it was only mostly hers.

That was where the letter signature's owner came in.

Hurb Fistic technically owned half the ships that docked in Sedrios. He was the sort of man whose business was simply moving money around without ever having to hammer a nail, stoke a fire, or tug a rope. On principle, Pickett had no problem with the concept of moneylenders. But Hurb Fistic was a moneylender like a mountain lion was a cat. A single missed payment was all it took for him to seize the whole of an asset, no matter how close the loan was to being paid off.

And her loan, well . . . She might have owned the building, but it had been far from ready to function as a bar. It needed a back room and new boardwalks. The floor and walls needed patching. The door itself was in good shape, but it needed new hinges if it were to function as a door. All of that came before the cost of doing business. Plus, the inventory—rum, beer, wine, bread—customers would exchange for coin had to be purchased. Pickett didn't have a shim to her name after purchasing the wretched building. So she had no choice but to make a deal with a moneylender. It was the only chance she had to live the independent life she craved.

Pickett paced back and forth, narrowing her eyes at the scrawl of the text in front of her, peppered with phrases such as *investment in the value of a waystation for traders* and *concern over the tardiness of the last repayment.*

And then, the dreaded words *transition from quarterly to monthly payments for the protection of business interests.*

Edie must have noticed Pickett's agitation, because she left Letterboy cooing over the not precisely dead fish to join her side. "What is it, Pickett?"

It was only three days late and only because Pickett had discovered a hole in the store room leading straight down into the murky water that needed immediate repair. Just another expensive problem on top of debt she'd accrued doing just that. And now Fistic wanted to switch her to monthly payments? Pickett could feel an invisible noose tightening around her neck.

"Eeeyow!" Letterboy howled, yanking his hand out of the bucket. The dead fish hung on with tiny, needle teeth. One empty eye socket twitched with the movement of a nonexistent eyeball.

Stupid impulsive just-like-her little shit!

"Stop that!" Pickett shouted, lunging for Letterboy before he could fling the fish to the floor and ruin the closest thing Pickett had to an act.

Edie eyes grew wide as Pickett grabbed the thing's slimy body, her palms sliding off it again and again as she tried to free the stupid child.

"What are you doing?" Edie demanded over Letterboy's

shouts that were starting to devolve into tears as he jerked and tugged.

At last, Pickett yanked a rag from the top of the bar and wrapped it around the fish. It bucked and writhed under the cloth, but before its slimy skin could soak the rag through, she managed to get enough of a grip to pull it free. It all but hissed, its jaw working violently. Pickett wrinkled her nose and dropped it back into the bucket.

Letterboy crumpled onto the floor, clutching a bleeding hand to his chest as he sniffled. Snot and tears were smeared across his face. Edie hurried to his side.

"Well, you ought to know better," Pickett chided. "Don't stick your hands in strange buckets."

Edie shot her a glare as she knelt down next to Letterboy, tutting softly. "I think you'll need a surgeon for that." She reached into her bodice.

Did she think they had surgeon money? Pickett thought but had the wisdom to keep it to herself.

Edie pulled out another pip, stuffing both the money and a piece of honey cake from the bar into Letterboy's good hand.

"Straight to the surgeon with you. Get that looked at. And keep your hands where they belong. Do you hear?"

Letterboy nodded and Edie stroked his hair until his tears slowed. With a loud sniff, he shoved the whole cake into his mouth, chewing miserably as crumbs fell to his filthy shirt. Then he scurried out of the bar.

Pickett huffed and planted her hands on her hips. "Edie, those coins were for your new shoes. Or do you want to walk around with a hole in your sole forever?"

Edie rose and brushed out her skirts.

"What use is having money if you don't use it for something worthwhile? I'd rather Letterboy keep his finger. Now I'm going to see if I can get something cooked that we can serve tonight. Full customer stomachs mean full bar coffers."

"I thought we were going to serve cake tonight."

"That was the last good one." Edie shrugged. "A rot got into the others. It happens. I'm going to make swamp crab stew."

Pickett wrinkled her nose. The swamp crabs accessible around their little corner of the swamp had about as much meat on them as a dragonfly. But they were slow and easy to catch, even if they were hard to spot at first. Their color shifted to any of a variety of shades of brown to match the color of the dingy waters. Pickett had once kept one up on the bar for an hour, watching its colors shift as it tried to catch the exact shade of stained brown as the wood. She couldn't really object to Edie's meal. They had to eat something, and they had to make money. She watched Edie go, a sour feeling settling in her stomach. What use was money? A better question was what use was it to have a bar and a shelter if its days were numbered. She glared down at the dead fish flopping around in the bucket.

"You'd better fix this tonight," she muttered.

The dead fish writhed violently, sending a splash of fetid water her way.

FOUR

Traders usually stopped by in the evenings, when the swamp air grew heavy and cool. It was a safe place to escape the dusk time bite of the bugs or else to warm up before continuing with the rest of the journey. Pickett had done all she could since she'd purchased the old fishing shack to turn it into the sort of place that people might actually stop amidst journeys. So far, the dice games she'd offered to them proved both a blessing and a curse. Sure, the traders bought more ale and rum when they were focused on the game, but they also blew more steam and tempers than her poor, rotting bar could afford. At least two stools moldered away at the bottom of the swamp, and more than a few stains on the floor came from a bloodied nose. Pickett could always blow a trick to frighten them into submission, but clay pots, mirrors, and explosives were not cheap.

That evening, as traders shuffled in to see Romona or at least Kellum's impersonation of her, more than a few scowled at the lack of performance going on. They lumbered up to the bar, dropped their pips and shims on the counter, and took their drinks to the tables to hunt down the dice. Nobody even paused to ask why Pickett had a bucket on the stage where there might have otherwise been a performer. At this rate, they were just going to sit around, get drunk, and cause more damage than what they'd paid for their drinks.

Useless old codgers.

Aside from the dice-players, the Northfellow sat in his usual spot at the corner of the bar, muttering to himself as he picked pond scum from his beard. Then there were a handful of people likely lingering only because they could smell swamp crab stew simmering in the kitchen. As soon as they ate what Edie prepared, they'd be gone. They'd bought meager beers, which they nursed without interest in the meantime. Pickett had until the stew came out to wring a few more coins from them.

Pickett cracked her knuckles, rolled her shoulders, and nodded to herself before bounding up to the stage. Ignoring Edie's disapproving glances, she flourished her colorful cape and brought her hands together, palms bent to release a clap like thunder ripping through the bar.

A couple of traders glanced up, then turned back to their beers. At least they enjoyed what she was serving.

"Good people, I have procured for you a marvel of magic's making," she announced. "My most recent forays into the mystic arts have unveiled to me a series of heretofore hidden and magnificent truths blinded from the eyes of humanity."

"What?" one of the traders called out, a portly fellow with a mustache like a rosy caterpillar and a name to match. Slurne tugged his pipe from his lips and gestured at the stage. "What're you gonna do, summon a demon or summat in that bucket?"

Pickett narrowed her eyes but raised her chin.

"Perhaps I would be better suited to summon your regular companion. The fisherman? Mole-lip?"

"Arn!" Slurne flushed a little on behalf of his friend.

"Well, be grateful that he wasn't here when I did my

summoning or I might've summoned only the truth that you cheated him at dice."

Laughter rumbled around the bar as Slurne buried his face in his glass. Pickett cleared her throat. "With gentle experimentation, my friends, I have done that which I knew not before that which magic would permit me to do. For a low low fee of two—"

"One!" Edie cried from behind the bar.

Pickett narrowed her eyes then sucked in a sharp breath. "One pip, you may gaze upon aquatic life, snuffed out, now returned from that foul brink to swim among us once again."

Laughter rose from the audience again, and Pickett's heart sank as not one of them rose to the bait. Traders and troubadours alike turned back to their drinks and their dice.

All but for the Northfellow, who sat up and stared intently at her with bright eyes beneath his shaggy brows. He slid off his stool at the bar and wove toward the stage, tugging at his white beard and muttering to himself in Andoshi. Without lifting his chin to meet her gaze, he shoved a coin into Pickett's hand before he crouched down in front of the bucket.

"My boys and I, we saw fish just like this in the forest with the dark gathering all around us . . ." then he trailed off, switching into the strange, exotic language of the people who chose to live in the ass-freezing north.

Pickett glanced down at her palm. A silver scale. A whole silver scale just to look at a dead fish. Edie might disagree with Pickett's methods, but she'd sure appreciate still having a roof over her head.

Pickett grinned and glanced down, watching him coo at the dead fish like it was a newborn baby. Creepy. But maybe that was just a Northish thing with their weird relationships with fish. She heard they ate them rotted, after all. Not that she could trust the word of traders any more than they could trust her.

Of course, if the Northfellow wanted to scoop the fish out of that bucket and dance a jig with it, Pickett would clap the beat. So long as she had coin in her pocket and her current entertainment survived, he could do anything short of ferment and eat it.

Gazes began to drift toward the stage. Traders and fishermen murmured to each other, even as Edie came out with the night's vittles: swamp crab stew and fresh bread. How she managed to scratch together something that actually smelled appetizing, Pickett wasn't sure. But somehow, even with their meager spices, Edie had pulled it off. That was just her way. Maybe Edie was the real swamp witch.

Between the pair of them, the patrons of Pick's Pocket didn't stand a chance. Half of them flocked to the stage, curious enough to shed a little coin to see the unnatural thing that so held the attention of the mad Northfellow. The other half flocked to Edie, the straw-haired siren in an old, embroidered corset bearing anything at all edible.

One by one, the pips dropped into Pickett's bag, each one of them like a fresh drop of blood fueling her—and this whole place. Pickett caught her breath. One bronze after another, bit by bit, she would be able to pay off Fistic, save enough for future costs, and build something that looked like a future for herself and, well, Edie.

The Northfellow kept his spot by the side of the bucket, but the others crowded around. Pickett made sure they were never quite close enough for the wretched thing to bite them. After what happened with Letterboy, Pickett didn't want Edie to offer refunds—or maybe even a free dinner—to whomever suffered a wound from her infernal pet.

One of the patrons, a traveling performer with shells wound in her hair, asked Pickett, "Back home, I have a cat. He's old, but he jumps through hoops. Quite a show at the local festivals. Think you can keep him alive like this fish, madame sorceress?"

Pickett wrinkled her nose. "Trust me. You'd rather your cat not be like this little bugger, eh?"

The performer glanced in the bucket and wrinkled her nose without answering.

Edie, meanwhile, swooped around the tables, collecting coin and spooning out bowls of swamp crab stew. The whole place smelled warm with whatever spices she'd dug up to season the thing. Pickett had to hold her breath before the spell broke and Pick's Pocket returned to being the chilly, crumbling dive it really was. For the moment, there was food, there was drink, and most importantly there was money enough to make her debt payment.

Slurne sidled up next to her, his great mustache twitching.

"Dead fish is impressive." He grunted, then nodded at Edie. "But I'd say the bigger trick is how you roped a pretty thing like that into your service. Arn told me she came on her own. You a magnet for sun-haired foreigners and the sort?"

Pickett grinned, more to herself than anything. Hexes. Demonic deals. Bargains for firstborns. Nobody would believe Edie showed up on her own then decided to stay. Pickett herself didn't quite believe it, but there she was, doling out stew, picking up coin, and brightening the whole place with her smile. Sure, Edie wasn't entirely rainbows and sunshine, even if she was the only one who knew it—and boy was she lucky to be the only one who did—but still. A creature like her, sharp edges and all, in a place like this. Yeah. Things were all right. Life could be shit, but sometimes it was actually kind of all right.

For just one more night, Pick's Pocket had food. It had drink. It had entertainment. It had Edie and it had *life*.

Soon enough, everyone who wanted a peek had their fill of the fish. Everyone save for the Northfellow, that was. He still sat whispering to the bucket, his eyes bright. Pickett was tempted to herd him back to his stool, but it didn't look like he was going to cause any trouble. If an undead fish brought him a little joy, well, who was Pickett to drag him away?

She sidled up to Edie behind the bar, dumping her coins into the money box next to the rum.

"We seem to be having a good night," she said airily. "So much for bad omens."

"For now," Edie said, leaning against the counter, but she began chewing on one of her thumbs. It was a habit she'd picked up a little after she showed up at the bar, whenever she thought of her shitty little village or the circumstances that had driven her from it. Pickett took a deep breath, grasping Edie's wrist, pressing it to the bar counter before Edie could draw blood.

They wouldn't discuss the matter of the fish openly, of course. It wouldn't help Pickett's reputation any to reveal that she had not, in fact, brought a dead fish back to life. Nor would it please anyone to know that it had simply flopped out of the swamp. But that didn't mean she needed to pretend nothing at all was wrong.

"Some trick," a trader muttered, shuffling up to the bar and slamming a wooden mug down. Pickett noticed a slight bulge in his wrist and clenched her teeth. Cheater dice. It had been too good to hope, after seeing how many went after the game.

"It's my specialty," she said, drumming her fingers against the bar counter. "As is knowing the truth in things. I like honest games in my establishment, sir."

"Mm," the trader mumbled, the blood draining from his face as he shoved his mug forward. The cheater dice spilled out. A little bashfully, he stuffed them in his pocket.

Edie pulled a face as she leaned over to refill the trader's beer. As he stumbled off to hopefully not piss off every other gambler in the bar, Edie's eyes flicked back to the bucket.

She really was like a very paranoid dog with a bone, wasn't she? Things were dumped into the swamp from time to time. Who was to say some strange potion or other hadn't simply fallen in and bewitched a single dead creature? Pickett had to remind herself of that over and over and over. Real magic was rare. Rarer still to show up for people like them. Rarest of all to actually be significant. Soon enough, whatever charm or potion that had caused the fish incident was bound to wear off with Pickett all the richer and Edie all the humbler.

After all, if the swamp crabs still smelled safe to eat, why should they have anything to fear from those waters?

The first indication was the sound of a splash on the half-rotted wooden planks. Then the acrid smell of vomit cutting through the air like a swift slap. The trader sagged against the bar, his cheek going a sickly sort of greenish yellow as he let out a guttural moan. Then came another heave and a splash. Slurne sagged in his seat, the sick dripping from his mustache.

Pickett's eyes widened. Fuck. Ever-hating fish-fucking fuck!

This was followed by another, this time from one of the traders. And another. A few managed to scramble for the door, clutching their mouths and stomachs to try and empty their guts into the swamp instead. Each and every one of them had purchased a bowl of the swamp crab stew. The odor that filled the bar was a mockery of the warm, homey smell the stew had first filled the space with.

Edie scowled and pulled the moneybox away from Pickett, already counting out a handful of coins.

"Bad omens indeed," Edie muttered.

Pickett glowered at her. But for the life of her, she couldn't summon a word sharp enough to fling back.

Refunds. No worse omen in the world than a refund.

CHAPTER

FIVE

alf the night's profits went back into the pockets of traders, troubadours, and disgruntled merchants. That left Pickett with just over four pips of actual profit for the night. With what she'd made off of Kellum and what she had in reserve, she could just pay Fistic for the month. Afterward, she'd have barely enough left for food, supplies, rum, beer, and the inevitability of more little disasters she'd need to fix. The odds that she could make the next payment on a monthly payment were about as likely as growing wheat straight out of the swamp. A bad month could be salvaged if it was followed by a good one. But if one bad month led to a missed payment, then she was fucked as a springtime rabbit. She needed to get back onto the quarterly payments, which demanded a little in-person charm.

If Pickett were a pettier person, she might've blamed Edie for their financial troubles. That stew disaster had wiped out the night's profits. But even if she screwed her face and willed her heart to turn to stone, she just couldn't be angry. Not at Edie, sweet Edie who'd given a coin of her own to patch up Letterboy's finger. Edie, who'd spent the day catching swamp crabs and digging the meager meat out from their shells so she could cook a decent stew. Edie, who smiled and brought sunlight into even the dingiest corners of the Pick's Pocket.

Pickett could certainly blame Edie. But Edie had been able to turn half-rotted vegetables and stale bread into a profitable dish before. She'd even served swamp crab stew before. Whatever happened, it wasn't Edie's fault.

Dammit.

She could blame Edie like she could blame the wind for blowing.

Pickett hunched over the bar, knocking back a thumb of rum. It burned like sweet, punishing fire, a welcome reprieve from the lingering reek of sickness in the air, the smell alone that had driven the non-vomiting patrons out, making even the swamp fragrant in comparison. Despite the last hour with the doors open and scrubbing all the pukish piles, the air was slow to clear from the stench.

Pickett glanced to her left, at the only other companion left at the bar. The Northfellow slumped in his seat, clutching a wooden flagon of whatever they'd had on hand. He wasn't picky. He still muttered to himself, swaying and occasionally humming a strange tune as foreign to Pickett's ears as his home country. And yet, night after night, he found sanctuary here.

Maybe the swamp crab stew disaster had made her maudlin, but Pickett couldn't stop her mind from wandering out along those splintery walkways that stretched across the swamps. How many different souls walked them? What strange winds drove them into this stinking and inhospitable territory to seek comfort, trade, and shelter in her ramshackle little bar? And what would it mean to distant travelers like the Northfellow if it was taken away by the clutching fingers of someone who'd be content merely to let it rot into nothing for the loss of some coin.

They'd have to find someone else to sell them bad beer and provide a roof for barter and hastily assembled entertainment.

Pickett knocked back the last of her rum and rose, going to pat the Northfellow on the back. There were little threadbare patches in his coat, showing the shirt beneath. He stank of fish, moreso even than the average person traveling along these paths. Nobody who smelled like that or who occupied his own stool at a dive bar like this had anywhere else to go. He'd been her very first patron. With any luck, he'd one day be her last. Yeah, he belonged here just as much as she did.

He raised his head, chin wobbling, which made his whole beard bounce like a springy cloud as his foggy blue eyes locked onto hers.

"When the winter kills the berries of summer, what hope remains for jam?" he asked.

Pickett frowned and reached for his flagon, giving the leftover beer a sniff. Didn't smell like a rot had gotten into it. Good. They'd already poisoned half their patrons with stew. It wouldn't do for the drink to be off too.

"What was that then?" Pickett asked, sliding the flagon back.

The Northfellow took it and muttered something in his language as he swirled the beer inside, then took a sip. "It is a love song. What hope remains for jam?"

"Sounds like a sad song to me," Pickett mused.

The Northfellow wrinkled his nose as something shifted behind those eyes. It plucked at Pickett's chest in a way that would make Edie proud. She was always telling Pickett to be more sensitive. Hard not to be with him, though. A crazy old man far from his home spending night after night in the Pick's Pocket without even bothering to try to trade with the other patrons. What had brought him here? Why didn't he go somewhere else?

"All love songs are sad songs," he muttered, his tongue half-tripping over the words.

All love songs are sad songs. Pickett wasn't old by any stretch of the imagination but the way those words pummeled her heart made her feel as ancient as the sea itself. He was very right and very drunk all at once.

Whatever was swirling in his head must have built itself into a proper storm, because he leaped out of his chair, holding the flagon high as he shouted something that sounded like a bear trying to recite a limerick. At the end of his Andosh declaration, he tipped the flagon, dumping the remains of his beer onto the splintery floor.

Somehow, the addition of beer to the lingering stench did not improve the situation at all. Pickett wrinkled her nose at the fresh mess she had to clean up. With a snort, she snatched the flagon from his hand and nudged his ass with her boot.

"You'll be singing a sadder song if you keep carrying on that way in my bar." She warned. "Now scoot. You must have some-where else to go."

He turned around, planting one wrinkly, knobby-knuckled hand on her shoulder.

"Hold on to what you have," he said, his voice going deep and husky as tears glossed over his eyes.

Well that was enough of that. She had her own disaster to manage. If she tried to carry him too, she might just crumble.

"Yes, yes, I'm trying." Pickett sighed, shrugging his hand off. There'd be other nights to be kind to him. For the moment, she just needed to be alone with her bar and her mess. "Now go before I turn you into a frog."

CHAPTER
SIX

The key to a good lie was to retain just enough truth that even the most discerning audience would hesitate to call a bluff. For everything else, there was flash and misdirection. Pickett told people she'd make sparks with her fingers, and she did just that. A swish of a colorful cape stitched with mirrors would draw the eye away from the flint in her rings and the way she swiped them together. She could tell people she'd turn water into wine, if only she could keep them from noticing the dried bread soaked through with said wine that she slipped into a bowl of said water.

But some people couldn't be tricked.

Fistic could have, for all intents and purposes, a fully fledged sorceress capable of razing his whole enterprise to the ground, but that wasn't what he'd see. He'd still see a desperate urchin trying to keep her bar afloat, and that was all she could respond to. For men like him, money superseded compassion, awe, and even fear. If he believed Pickett was a desperate urchin, then he'd choke her out to eliminate a liability.

Her meager reserves weren't going to be enough to keep them in business. After the swamp crab stew incident, she couldn't count on much in the way of profits until she had a real draw again. She'd be lucky to earn a shim at this rate, and it certainly wouldn't be enough with Fistic's new payment schedule.

Pickett scowled and hunched over the bar, fiddling with one of her little clay tricks. This one was simple enough, shaped like a miniature pot the size of an eye and designed to break and release a cloud of thick dust. It produced enough to run away, or trick an idiot into thinking a fire was somewhere.

Footsteps creaked down the old, splintered stairs. Only months of practice stopped Pickett from reacting and hurling the "magic" device at the would-be intruder. Edie was doing a lot to make this place her own. If she wasn't careful, Pickett was going to get so used to it that she wouldn't know what to do without a companion.

"I've got the bedrolls rolled up but yours is about to develop another hole. I'll darn it when I get the chance." Edie poked her head through the door, a couple of hairs slipping down from her tangled bun. She rubbed one eye with the heel of her palm and frowned. "Why are you working on that? I haven't been to the chemist. Do you even have enough materials to make anything?"

"I'm clever enough. I've got the whole place rigged with mirrors and dust bombs, haven't I?" Pickett shrugged. "Besides. This one's not too expensive. I can make it from leftover powders. Enough if we need to spook off a rowdy customer."

Edie crossed her arms and leaned against the doorframe. In just her chemise, the little motion made the thin linen hug her barely present curves just right. Pickett might have averted her eyes, but she'd learned once that doing so was a certain way to draw unwanted attention to her, well, attention.

"Mirrors and dust bombs take time and money." Edie pointed out.

"I excel at producing both."

"Pickett, please." Edie strode forward, leaning onto the bar. Another loose, straw-blonde lock of hair fell into her face. Loose. Unprotected. Trusting. That was dangerous.

"Please what?" Pickett turned back to her task. Faking magic was mostly a matter of clever chemical work, which meant a delicate focus on fine powders and liquids poured into intentionally thin jars. It wasn't cheap, being a swamp witch. But it was convenient when one didn't want to look someone in the eyes. Being a woman running an establishment like this wasn't easy, but with her carefully crafted reputation, she'd been able to keep safe so far.

"Please tell me the truth," Edie urged. "Are we in trouble? We as in the bar, I mean."

It would have been so easy. Pickett could have just turned around right there and told her about Fistic. About the debt she'd taken on to turn the Pick's Pocket into a halfway-decent waystation in the Rottering swamps. She could tell her that a single missed payment would close them down for good and that making the payment would mean eating dirt unless they could make real money. That Pickett would go out of business and Edie would go back to being a foundling with no family, no fortune, and potentially no future.

No. Edie had been through too much. She'd been an orphan from a dingy backwater village, chased into the swamps by a murderer. In the end, Edie had done what she'd had to do. And Pickett couldn't turn her away. Not when she knew all too well how it felt to feel alone in the world. For all the comfort and hospitality Edie had brought to the Pick's Pocket, she deserved more than grief. Besides, Pickett was going to find a way around it. The bar was her place. Edie was her person, whether she realized it or not. It was up to Pickett to look after them both.

"I'm worried about the food situation." Pickett sniffed, scraping some of the pricey yellow powder into a thin bag. "Not for nothing, but there's probably a sickness going around. Not your fault but they're sure to blame it on the stew."

Edie furrowed her brows. "Pickett, I think we both know—"

"And," Pickett cut in, "we still need to have something to feed them. Drunks make bad customers. Hungry drunks make impossible customers. Especially when there's dice on the tables, but I can hardly take that away from them."

Edie hummed knowingly. "Dead drunks make dead business."

Pickett arched a brow. "You're learning from me a little too well, I think."

"Of course." Edie sauntered to the other side of the bar, climbing onto a chair right next to Pickett. She hunched her shoulders and leaned forward, staring straight at Pickett's eyes. "Pickett, you took me in, even when it was probably a stupid choice."

Pickett glared but Edie just shrugged. "No 'probably' about it. It was a stupid choice. Best stupid choice I ever made."

"You gave me a home. Put a roof over my head when I desperately needed one. You gave me a place I'd defend with everything I've got. You understand that, right?"

Oh, but Pickett did. All too well. If only she had actually been born with a knack for magic. If only all her lies could be truths, she'd never have to worry again. If she had any sort of magical, inhuman sorcery up her sleeve she could use to keep this place going, she'd take it. The best she had was mirrors and dust bombs and little bags and bottles of overpriced chemicals to convince people she ought to be taken seriously.

"Just trust me." Pickett settled on. "Just for a little longer. I've kept us going this long, eh?"

Edie arched a brow. "When we first met, you injured yourself smashing your face into your own bar."

"I was distracted."

"You were drunk."

"It was the planting season. Everyone gets drunk on Planting Day. Or whatever the backwaters in your little village called it." Pickett pulled the little bag closed and turned in her chair. "Helped you in the end, didn't I?"

Edie sniffed. "I did the heavy lifting. Literally."

"Yes, but I had the roof to supply." She patted her hand on the bar. "Trust me to keep that roof standing a while longer. When I go off on days like this, that's just what I'm doing. Keeping this place going."

Edie sighed. Then, like a petal blooming, she spread her fingers and settled her hand on Pickett's.

"You got me off topic. I'm trying to say we're together in this. You can share your burden with me, you know."

Did she know that? Edie had raced into this bar months ago, dirty and sweating and fleeing for her life. As far as Pickett knew, this bar was the first place Edie had truly been able to call a home. How would it benefit her to know she might be about to lose it? No, she'd been through enough. Pickett had made the stupid, impulsive, inebriated decision to let this strange young woman into her life. She'd just have to do her best not to break her heart.

"My burden at this moment"—Pickett slid the collection of little bags toward Edie—"is that I need to run an errand so I won't have time to build my tricks. I might not be back until tomorrow. Would you mind running the place on your own?"

Edie arched a brow but picked up one of the bags. "I should be able to do that. But if you're going into a town, take the fish with you."

"Why? It hasn't died properly has it?"

As if on cue, there came a thump from the barrel confirming that, no, the little beast was still alive—and still feisty.

"It's just an asshole," Edie said. "And it's starting to stink up my home."

Pickett smirked and patted Edie's knee. "The joys of swamp-living."

SOUTHFEN WAS HALF a day's journey southwest from the Pick's Pocket. When she arrived, Pickett would still have business to tend to. That was far too much to ask her to go entirely by foot. So she started her journey by easing herself slowly toward one of the nearby villages, betting on finding help. Sure enough, a vegetable cart with a father and son crossed paths with her. The child looked intrigued while the father regarded her warily.

"Afternoon, traveler," Pickett called, going up to pat the mule.

It regarded her warily as well. A firm but gentle scratch along its neck and the carrot hidden in her sleeve were enough to overcome its caution. It nuzzled at her wrist, great nostrils flaring until she pulled the vegetable out and fed it.

The father's expression softened. It was a simple trick that did nothing to prove that she was good or trustworthy, but people tended to relax around someone kind to their animals. A beast's judgment was better than a human's, as some people tended to say. Pickett didn't know if that was true, but it had won her plenty of free rides in her life.

"Heading to Southfen?" the farmer asked gruffly.

Pickett nodded and pulled a coin from her pocket. "I'd appreciate the chance to spare my legs. I can even take over steering for a little while if you want to rest."

And thus, she found herself in the back of a cart, nestled up against an assortment of onions and radishes, breathing in their reek as she stared up at the noon sky. The Rottering swamp always smelled worse in the heat of the day.

Edie would run the bar that night. There were enough jars of false smoke and pulleys to allow her to pull off any magic she needed to if anyone tried to hassle her. It might even help to convince some of the clientele that Pickett could protect the bar from anywhere. On top of that, Edie knew who to and not to serve, how to earn money. She probably wouldn't push the spectacle of the undead fish, which Pickett refused to take with her, but that likely only had a few weeks of interest in it, anyway. Whether Edie liked it or not, at the moment it was the only draw they had to attract those who would just as soon drink alone in their homes. Something squirmed in Pickett's gut at the knowledge that she wouldn't be back by nightfall. For once, she hoped for low traffic. The idea of Edie having to handle some of their worst clientele without backup didn't sit well at all.

The little boy twisted around, half hanging over the back of the cart as he stared at her with wide, brown eyes. "Papa says you're a swamp witch."

"Ssh!" his father hissed.

But Pickett grinned, turning to face the boy. "It's perfectly fine. I am."

"How do you get to be like that?"

"Oh, you know"—Pickett shifted, making herself comfortable against the bags of onions—"a little bit of a lot of things. Bit of born with it. Bit of practice with it. Bit of luck when it came to learning to get better."

"Oh." The boy dug his finger in his nose. "Where'd you come from?"

"All over," she said airily. "Greenshade mostly." Which wasn't exactly a lie, but it was close enough that Edie would call it one. But people around here were unlikely to have ever been out to Greenshade enough to call her on her bluff. And if they did, she'd risk the even bigger lie of being from up north by the Troll Coast.

"Can you do swamp magic now?"

Pickett shrugged and plucked a radish from a bag, bouncing it between her hands. "Wouldn't be a good idea. Traveling like this means we aren't in one place. Confuses the waters. You don't want confused waters when you do magic." She winked at him.

The father tugged on the boy's shirt. "Leave her be, child." Then he leaned down and whispered, just loud enough for Pickett to overhear, "If we're good to her, perhaps she'll offer a fine enchantment."

Fine enchantments. Blessings. Good fortune. Pretty words to make people feel better, but they tended to appreciate the good feelings and they were far less troublesome than powders and mirrors.

Pickett snuck in a nap before it was her turn to drive the cart, shooing the boy back to rest with his father. Then back again after a few hours of travel. As the sun rose high enough to bring out the worst of the swamp stink, the first sight of Southfen swam into focus. Reeds and cattails marked the shallows as the boardwalk gave way to a gravelly path over thick shrubland, great wooden signs noting that Southfen was just ahead.

Pickett sat up and steeled her mind for what was to come.

Southfen sprawled out from the road like a glass of wine spilling from an open cup. Building after stone-shingled building peppered the stone-and-gravel roads. Great masts sang and swung beyond them, the sound of sailors and ship bells dominating all other sounds of the city. This was where the rum boy got his spirits. This was the heart of her business. Most of the traders in the Pick's Pocket came from or headed to this city.

Pickett hopped out of the cart, patting the mule and clearing her throat. "May you serve your family well, and may you be more horse than ass."

The father inclined his head, but the boy wrinkled his nose. Well at least they'd have a fun story to share.

She wandered down the Southfen streets, passing some establishments typical of port towns: the Horny Serpent, the Grand Cat Scratch, and of course the Spotted Dick.

There was really no reason to have any sort of reaction to it, and yet Pickett's heart flipped like the dead fish back home. The Spotted Dick must have changed hands at least twice since she'd last been inside it, but the current proprietor must have something approaching good taste. The old stone building had a fresh wash of white paint on it. Someone had removed the old, rotting shutters, replacing them with sheer, crimson cloth laced with gold thread. It was far from the shabby old lean-to that her younger, more urchiny self had run to for shelter on a rainy night.

She remembered when the employees—Dick Dames they called themselves—hung out of the windows, their bodices tied to maximize the amount of cleavage visible as they shouted and coaxed sailors to spend a little coin on them. Once, a Dick Dame had been so bold as to allow the tiniest flash of nipple right there in the window. The resulting war between the whorehouses and the constabulary had made it into many a bard's song for months afterward. She had to dig deep into her mind to try and remember who the Dame had been to cause the ruckus. Tandy? Marie? Certainly not Flora. She caused enough trouble on her own that even a decade's time couldn't make Pickett forget. What she did remember was feeling safe in Madame's office, learning to balance the books and running errands and feeling safe. Until she hadn't.

Pickett placed a hand on the white wall. Were any of them still employed there? Or had they, like her, dispersed and tried to make their own homes in the world?

She couldn't imagine any of the old Dames sticking around under the present circumstances. Some idiot was trying to turn the Spotted Dick into some sort of *respectable* establishment. Had they no shame?

And what would the place look like today if things had gone differently? If she'd chosen differently? Certainly she wouldn't be running a bar in a swamp, begging Fistic for money. Maybe she'd still be sitting in the dusty back room, dreaming of a life that looked deceptively close. Deceptively safe. But the dusty back room was probably different too.

Pickett had half a mind to go in, just to see how changed the interior was, and maybe even tell off whomever had thought to paint over such a historical landmark. Fate interceded when a hand came to rest on her shoulder. She stiffened then stole a quick glance at the offending appendage. On his middle finger was a pewter ring with a crest: three coins above a schooner. Pickett recognized Fistic's official crest worn by him, his servants, and his enforcers.

"Master Fistic's been expecting you, Pickett." The huge man who towered over Pickett had a birth mark under one eye that looked like a daisy. Pickett might have snorted at that if he wasn't the size of a tree. Daisy-face jerked a thumb down the street, right at the most recognizable landmark in this part of the city. Anyone with eyes could see what was commonly called the Bully Building from a thousand feet away. A three-story stucco building with a faded pink wash and tidy yellow eaves. Like a toxic fish, it lured its victims in with pretty colors. But once they were inside, they met the shark of Southfen.

Pickett took a deep breath, then spun around, smirking. "Very good. I've been meaning to visit him too."

CHAPTER

SEVEN

Everything about Fistic's office bespoke luxury, from the plush chairs draped in satin to the thick swatches of plants hanging from the walls and ceilings to the half-dozen bird cages that peppered the place. Each bird had its own call, and they traded off warbling and crowing, twittering and chirping in a soft background roar that made Pickett's temples ache. How could someone work in an environment like this? It certainly said something about the money he could invest in maids that the place still smelled more like flowers than bird shit.

Not for the first time, she wished she could bounce back in time and slap some sense into her younger and stupider self. Nobody with this kind of wealth was to be trusted. Looking back, she was pretty sure Fistic had been all too aware that the bar was a bad idea and a money pit, but that money could flow right into his pocket as long as he kept the pump running. The younger, stupider Pickett hadn't known that "interest rate" did not mean the rich bastard was actually interested in her business.

Now she knew better, and it would be all too easy to turn

herself into an enemy. It took every ounce of self-control Pickett had to force herself to smile when she saw him. He had to like her. He had to cooperate with her.

Fistic himself stood next to a hanging plant laden with bright, orange flowers that resembled little cabbages, emptying a cup of water lovingly in the pot. He was a plump man, well-dressed in silks with dark curls carefully tamed into a tasteful coif. He'd have been handsome if not for the hunger that burned in his eyes. It was a look Pickett knew all too well, and she'd learned not to relax too much around anyone who had it. But she had to pretend to relax, pretend she was at ease. She was just a businesswoman speaking to a businessman, asking him to revert her payment schedule. *Nothing to worry about. Nothing at all. Keep it friendly. Keep him happy.* She could manage it.

He turned and smiled a little too toothily and gestured at one of the chairs. "Pickett! Wonderful to see you. I hope your journey wasn't too trying."

Pickett did not sit, so neither did Fistic.

"No trip is too trying when I know I'll be seeing a good friend at the other end."

Those hungry eyes glinted. Pickett doubted Fistic trusted flattery, but he certainly liked it all the same.

"Could I offer you something to drink? Tea, perhaps, or a juice?"

"Actually, I would love something to eat if you have it. Nothing too big. Just a bite." It was an old trick she'd learned from the days before she'd decided to become a booze-flinging swamp witch. One of the quickest ways to establish a friendly atmosphere was to ask for a small, reasonable favor. She didn't understand it, herself, but lending a book or offering a hand to someone somehow made a person fonder of them. And she needed Fistic to be fond of her.

He nodded and gestured to one of the guards. The burly man disappeared and returned a moment later with a silver dish stacked with little fish-shaped cakes that smelled like spice and orange water. Spicefish was the sort of delicacy only a well-to-do family could afford, and just the sight of them made her mouth water. Pickett genially popped one in her mouth, trying not to think of the dead fish smashing itself against the sides of the barrel back home. The little fucker was absolutely not going to ruin this for her, except that he already had. *Little prick.*

"Delicious," she said, smiling far too sweetly at him.

"Good. I aim to keep my friends happy." He leaned forward onto his desk and winked at her. "We are friends, aren't we?"

A dangerous question, especially with her repayment schedule on the line. Pickett rolled the dice in her head, gambling on the right answer.

"Good friends, I should say. I've treasured our ongoing relationship."

"And good friends look out for each other. So I must ask"—he pressed a hand to his chest and frowned—"why, my dear friend, have you not looked out for me?"

Brick shits, she'd rolled wrong. But she couldn't dare stop smiling. "I've always ensured you received your payments. Grateful as I am for your loan."

The bird in the cage behind Fistic began to squawk, darting around as it watched something just outside the window. Without sparing it a glance, Fistic smacked the cage, startling the creature into silence.

"Friends," he drawled, "especially good friends, as you put it, do not leave their friends wanting. Or hungry. Good friends, Pickett, are timely with their payments."

"And yet your pockets have never been empty."

"No." Fistic plucked one of the fish sweets from the plate, only to crumble it into pieces between his fingers, letting the crumbs fall in a mess onto the desk. Once his fingers were cleared, another burly guard came to sweep the mess away, albeit with a surly scowl. This was certainly a show of force.

Pickett itched to tug the flints from her sleeve but resisted the urge.

As his muscle departed, Fistic smiled unpleasantly and patted the pockets of his waistcoat. "I have never been without funds, certainly. But I know the heft of my pockets, and I know when they are light. In the interest of our friendship, I allowed you to pay quarterly. There are others whom I require to pay weekly. It's a sign of my esteem for you that I spare you the long trek in from the Rottering swamp."

"Is my consistency in paying it on our old schedule no longer sufficient? Friend?"

"Ah, but your payment is late. And you didn't bother to come and see me until my letter was received." He heaved a dramatic sigh and pinched a fingerful of fish cake, sprinkling it into the bird's cage. The little beast chirped softly and hopped down, pecking at it happily. Fistic sighed and toyed with one of his well-coiffed curls. "I appreciate the consistency of a good friendship. But when aspects of such a relationship are rendered inconsistent. Well perhaps a quarter is too long. Perhaps it is too much time to forget the significance of the money you owe. Too much time to imagine you're in a position to play with it. To forget your very good friendship." He turned back to her. "Perhaps it would be better if you were to abide by the same conditions I am able to offer to those here in Southfen. Monthly payments would make me feel more secure. Or else I have contacts in service. Indenture is a way to earn back missing payments."

Brick shits. Brick shits filled with spiders and spikes and stinging scorpions.

Pickett wrinkled her nose and gave him a queasy smile. "That would be asking me to think in the short term. And nobody with such a menagerie"—she gestured at the many bird cages, earning a few squawks and shaken feathers in return—"could possibly be the sort of person prone to thinking in the short term. Monthly payments will ruin my profits and if you take out an indenture contract, then I won't be able to make any money from the bar."

"Perhaps. So what long term advantages can you offer me?"

Pickett arched a brow. "A fabulous act. One of a kind. It's the sort of act that people will come back again and again to see. Even those who might not otherwise. Why, soon enough I'll be such a fine establishment that even the townsfolk unprudish enough to venture to the swamp for sport will come to see it."

"Goodness me, what a promise." Fistic ran his fingers along the smooth wood of his desk. "And what sort of progress have you had?"

The truth would screw her up like a jagged screw, but a lie could be just as dangerous. Last time Pickett had rolled for the truth, it had turned out poorly. So maybe it was a good time to swing her odds in the other direction.

"Don't dare say, yet. But she's magnificent. Charisma from her tits to her toes." All right. She had to pause. Roll the dice again. Hard to read the actual roll but it felt like enough deception to be safe. "And shy." She thought back to Kellum's performance. "But funny! Funny enough for drunk merchants to grow loose with their coin. Funny enough for them to come back."

"Funny you say?" He leaned forward onto his knuckles and quirked a brow. "I last heard new roads might be built. Dirt roads are faster than wooden planks and far less treacherous. Cheaper to maintain too. Is your new act truly entertaining enough to tempt merchants onto those boardwalks after they're offered an alternative?"

Fuck. If Fistic was talking about it, then it must be true. A new road was coming to cut into her business. Pickett forced a shrug. It felt like lifting bricks with her bare shoulders. "You're always welcome to see for yourself, of course. The Pick's Pocket is welcome to any friendly soul who passes through the door. Especially my friends."

"Perhaps I will. It sounds like quite a novelty. I've never known Ms. Ovlovey to be prone to humor." At last, Fistic plopped down into his chair, twining his fingers together in a smooth, well-practiced gesture. "Can you tell me one of her jokes?"

Pickett clenched her teeth, tightening her tense grin. "My performer's humor is in song. And I sing like a cat with a cracked throat. Not something I'd want to subject your poor ears to."

"Interesting that you haven't named your performer." Fistic mused, twisting a ring on one of his fingers. "I last heard that Ms. Ovlovey had permanently migrated here to Southfen. As she puts it, the atmosphere of Pick's Pocket was not up to her standards, and the audience left much to be desired. So forgive me if I doubt your word."

Pickett planted both her hands on the desk, her lip curling. "Fuck Ovlovey five ways to a good fondle. I was one big shot. Her current benefactor is her next. One more ancient rich man or foolish heir and she'll be done singing for good."

"All the same, I have reasonable concerns. A tavern in the middle of a swamp that won't rent rooms. A generous quarterly payment expected and still you're late. And now your certain draw to convince traders it's worth their time to stop a few hours is, well, whoring herself out in Southfen, if you'd risk your reputation on such a rumor."

Scorpion shit. Maybe she should have brought Edie after all. The stupid, sweet-talking darling.

"Yes." Pickett mimicked him, leaning forward onto the desk. "I have every confidence in my new draws. Soon enough, we'll be fighting to keep others from building in the swamp."

"Mm. I heard a rumor that you'd found a swamp beast and wrangled it into a bucket."

Pickett grimaced, thinking of the foul-tempered fish. It was a small surprise that he'd already heard about it, but traders did talk. "Of a sort. I've decided to branch out into different attractions. Curiosities and the like. A guaranteed success."

"What a lovely idea. But of course with Miss Orlovey's departure, I have reason to feel concern for my investment. The fact that you came to discuss the matter in person only furthers my concerns that you are unable to make the payments on the new schedule."

"Not at all," Pickett replied. "I just think it's a tacky thing to do, suddenly changing the terms of the loan on a whim and a rumor."

"Whims and rumors are more powerful than you think," Fistic pointed out. "And you've made me nervous. So I'll need some degree of insurance. As a promise of sorts that I need not call in the whole of the loan now."

Fuck. "Name it."

"Oh don't sound so dour, Pickett." Fistic leaned back in his chair, raising an arm and sapping without ever removing his eyes from hers. Footsteps pounded and a door opened and closed. Fistic dragged a notepad out of a drawer. "By my ledgers, the fairest estimation feels like a gentle reassurance. The sort I'd offer to a friend. You need only pay a week early."

A week early? Pickett's heart froze. She thought of the fish slamming itself against the barrel. How much money could it honestly make until Kellum returned?

"A week early is a vice upon my time." She hissed, flicking her fingers together, sparks flicking into the air.

Fistic shrugged, not even bothering to glance at the sparks. "I could be persuaded to keep you on your current schedule. Of course, whatever down payment you have on you would help in that regard. And a 30 percent fee. Though I will be sending another friend along afterward to check on things."

Robbery! Pickett bristled. "Friendly or not, I can turn you into a frog."

The doors opened again, and another burly servant came into

the room, holding a cup and tray of steaming tea. Fistic didn't even tear his eyes from her as he accepted.

"Perhaps you can. Friend." He blew on the cup, then took a sip. "But if I am to be a frog, I will still be a rich frog. And your magical, indentured ass will still be without the Pick's Pocket."

SO MUCH FOR getting back on the old payment schedule. If Pickett had the means to truly curse the bastard, she'd do it just for the pleasure, even if her circumstances remained woefully inert. Could it be that Fistic suspected the truth? Or was he simply arrogant enough not to care? Even if she could turn him into a frog, Fistic could probably arrange for fat grubs and a fine indoor pond. And where would Pickett be?

Well, she'd make it somehow. She'd sweep her shattered heart into a bag and haul it around like she always did. But what about Edie? Poor thing had shown up half starved. In the months she'd worked there, she'd plumped up. Hard to say how, given their slim food budget, but she had all the same. And she smiled more than she had those first few days. Edie couldn't go back to her piss pot of a town, and Pickett couldn't ask her to pick up shop and travel around, homeless and hungry for opportunity. It had been a reckless and impulsive and perhaps inebriated decision to let Edie in on her secret of fake witchery. Now Pickett had someone else to worry for, and she didn't do a good enough job tending to herself.

She needed money, not just on time but early.

If she had the stones for it, she'd pop back into the Spotted Dick and see if she could ask for help, but there was no knowing who was in charge anymore. She no longer knew who was safe to approach for a loan or who might just gut her on the spot. Choosing the wrong lender last time was exactly how she'd gotten into this mess in the first place.

"If ever a filly were ever fucked, then how much luck for a filly or a buck?" she muttered to herself, stuffing her hands in her pockets as she strutted down the street.

If she lingered at the edge of town long enough, she could catch a ride back to Pick's Pocket. And if she was lucky, maybe she could formulate a fresh plan before she arrived home. Maybe she wouldn't be forced to tell Edie anything other than the day's biscuit quota. Not that she needed to do even that. It had been Edie who'd started providing reliable food, after all.

Pickett wandered to the edge of town. The cakes from Fistic's men still sank heavy in her gut. She doubted she'd be able to eat again until she was home.

As she sank down onto a rocky outcropping, she tugged her worry coin from one of her pockets. It had been old, all features worn off well before it had come into her possession. Finger to finger, knuckle to knuckle she bounced it, counting the seconds, the moments, the possibilities. A road was coming in soon, and Fistic wanted his money sooner. Ovlovey was gone. Kellum could only come every couple of weeks. A fish was only going to be worth a couple of viewings until everyone grew bored of it.

Finger to finger, knuckle to knuckle, she bounced the coin, willing a solution to materialize itself. What she got instead was a gardener with a week's worth of dirt under his fingernails and the faint scent of manure clinging to him like a fog.

"Miss? You the swamp witch, miss?"

She looked him up and down. Either he was an extremely clever con man—in which case he was smarter than she was and probably had backup plans to screw her over—or else he was just a gardener who wanted the help of a presumed magic user. The latter was more likely and, after her failed meeting, she was done trying to be clever.

"Yeah?" she said, sitting up straighter. "What d'you want?"

The gardener took a step back, then reached deep into his

pocket, tugging out a little pouch that clinked faintly. "I need you to have a look at someone for me."

The clink of coins was certainly tempting, but even if Pickett had been tempted to be that sort of dishonest, Edie sang in the back of her mind in her damned inconvenient warm and comfortable voice, urging her to be kind over pragmatic.

"I'm not a healer," she said, staring down at the coin bouncing from finger to finger, knuckle to knuckle.

"Don't need a healer, miss. I need a . . . Well I suppose I need an assessment of sorts."

Well that didn't sound so morally dubious.

The next thing Pickett knew, she stood in front of a small, thatch-roofed house on the outskirts of town, where the grocers were few and the fleas were doubtless substantial, but she had the promise of half the offered pouch of coin as well as a ride back home when her assessment was finished, which felt like a fair deal.

"My boy Jonrie's been peculiar lately."

Pickett arched a brow. "Mm. And how old is he?"

"Twelve. Just turned a week ago."

"Well then, peculiar's par for the course. Nobody needs a swamp witch for puberty."

"It's not . . ." The gardener huffed and gestured at the house. "Just go in. It'll be you two. His ma's serving on a merchant ship. I promised her I'd get an answer before she returned. About whether or not he had your . . ." He wiggled his fingers, which Pickett translated as his way of saying "magic."

One way or another, it was a free trip back to Pick's Pocket. Pickett pushed into the thatched house. In the corner knelt a pre-adolescent boy, his hair tied in two dozen tight braids, each topped with a glass bead, courtesy of his sailor mother, no doubt. When he saw her, he jumped to his feet, reaching into his pocket.

So that's how it was.

Pickett took a step forward, making sure to flare her colorful cape as she did.

"I am the swamp witch," she announced. "Your father has hired me to assess your magical abilities, Jonrie."

Jonrie froze, but the loose linen of his pants trembled down near his ankles.

"Oh. Um. Certainly, miss." He pulled his hands out of his pockets and went to the desk.

His parents must have been prosperous indeed. Despite the humble home, he pulled out a pen, inkwell, and a scrap of paper. Pickett arched a brow.

"You know your letters?"

"That's how Mother and Father got to know each other. She taught him and he taught me." He uncorked the inkwell and dipped the pen in before scribbling on the page.

Pickett sniffed the air thoughtfully. Citrus. Interesting. "Is your mother a merchant in the Paradisals?"

Jonrie paused, then continued. "It's the closest trading spot to Sedrios, isn't it?"

Pickett sighed. Kid didn't know shit, did he? She could relate. They'd all been young, once, and even as well-off as he was, she doubted he knew much geography.

So she shrugged. "Yes. Good trading spot. Definitely not dangerous at all."

Jonrie straightened, holding out a page. Despite his scribbling, it remained blank.

Pickett snorted. "As if you wrote nothing at all."

For the first time, Jonrie's lip twitched. "But I did. It's my-my magic," he explained, taking a step back and holding the paper up to a lantern. After a second, the words began to appear, darkening just before the paper did.

Pickett couldn't help smirking.

There once was a lonely old maid

In whose bed every bach'lor had laid.
Though the ladies did scorn
They'd do better to mourn,
For none knew just whose husbands had paid.

"Rotten poetry," she mused. "Would you believe I knew the poet?"

"Mother said it was written in Southfen."

"It was." She gestured at the paper. "You'd do well to stop fooling everyone. A real swamp witch knows a con by its sight."

Jonrie's face fell, but not long enough to display true disappointment. He must have seen this coming. How could he not?

"Clever recipe." She gestured at the inkwell. "But you might want to hide the smell of the citrus. Maybe find a substitute. It gave you away."

"Will you tell my father?"

"No, you will." Pickett gathered her cloak around her and sighed, looking the boy up and down. "You knew you'd be caught."

"It was just a prank," he said. "I wanted to surprise them. Make them happy. Mother had been gone a good while and then they were fighting."

All too old a tale. Pickett grimaced and stepped forward, leaning down to look Jonrie in the eye. "Listen, idiot. Sorcery is demon stuff. It's scary and dangerous and not worth dabbling in unless you're certain you can scare everyone around you into leaving you alone."

"I . . ." He flushed. "It was only for my folks."

"Demon stories spread. Magic isn't safe shit." Pickett leaned forward and narrowed her eyes. "You shouldn't put yourself in peril for such a reason. It's good to want to cheer them up. But it's a fool's plan to light yourself on fire to give them warmth."

Jonrie lowered his eyes and bit his cheek, but nodded. "I'll-I'll tell him." He promised.

"Good." Pickett shrugged. "And maybe ridiculous poems will be enough to ease their moods. And if they aren't? Still not your job, kid."

Jonrie dipped his chin, his shoulders jerking in a half-shrug. It was as close as she'd get to an agreement for one night.

"Come on," she said, shrugging, flicking her cape. "Lead me back outside with your head held high. A good con is nothing to be ashamed of."

To young Jonrie's credit, he did just that. Chin held high. Shoulders back. There was a tremor in his hands, but he didn't let it slow him down. Pickett ambled away just a few paces, not wanting to risk what was likely to be an awkward moment between father and son.

It was probably for the best. Her business would be truly screwed if she actually did stumble upon a real sorcerer in these parts.

As she kicked her way through the weedy grasses, a soft banging filled the air, like a hammer on a fence. She frowned, glancing left, then right, then down.

A frog sat in a small, wooden cage, but only for a moment. It flung itself at the woven slats of the cage. How it knew where to fling itself, she did not know. Its eyes were two goopy holes. It was missing a leg and its whole color was wrong, more gray than green or brown or any color a frog ought to be.

She knelt down. It lowered itself to the ground, opening its mouth to let out an odd, wet hiss. Not very frog-like at all. Then again, how many fish were known to fling themselves up out of the water and bite at messenger boys?

"Were you a pet?" she asked, tilting her head to one side. "Or are you an oddity like my little fellow back home?"

The frog trembled, then launched itself forward again. Whatever its origins, it probably hadn't been like this before.

"Fuck." Pickett sighed, leaning back on her heels. Edie was going to be so smug when she heard.

CHAPTER

EIGHT

S o long, fishie," Pickett announced solemnly "We wish we knew you better."

"Not really," Edie added. "Are you sure we should just put it back?"

"This is where it came from in the first place," Pickett pointed out. "Besides, do you know any demon sorcerers who can study it?"

"Well no, but . . ." Edie shrugged. "I wanted it gone, but it just feels weird to wash our hands of this."

"Well, for lack of anything else coming to mind."

Pickett crouched low to dump the dead fish back into the swamp. It tumbled out of the bucket, jaws gnashing as it splashed into the water, a slimy handful of smelly fury. And with him went all her foreseeable hopes. And to think, this time a day ago her hopes had been so high. The stink of the evening swamp water was more rank than ever.

"Good riddance." Edie gathered up her skirt and sank down, lithe and graceful as a willow, and let her feet dangle over the edge. Pickett could just spy the soles of Edie's shoes where they'd tried to peel away, which she'd had to repair with an awl

66

and some thick twine. The leather was so thin in one spot she could almost spot Edie's stocking. Those shoes needed replacing badly.

So she'd lost the fish. She'd lost Ovlovey. Kellum wouldn't be back until it was too late, and even if he came early, there'd be no getting the word out and attracting enough of a crowd to make the money in time.

Money, money, money. There'd been a time when Pickett loved money. Now she hated it. Perhaps she ought to fuck off into the woods and become a forest witch. Surely forest witches could set up shop without having to buy and maintain property, not to mention the overhead of buying and selling booze.

Pickett must have let some inkling of her worry slip onto her face, because Edie leaned over, giving her a shove.

"Hey," she said. "What's the difference between a priest and a libertine?"

"What?"

"A priest and a libertine. What's the difference?"

Pickett sighed and leaned back on her hands. "Well. They're both drunk on their own abilities to sway people. Both the sort of person to live on the power of reputation."

Edie pulled a face. "Pickett, you're ruining it."

"I know, that's the point. I don't want to hear some idiot joke you picked up from a merchant. They aren't half as clever as they think they are."

Edie nudged Pickett with one foot. "Humor me."

"Humor's stretching it."

"What's the difference between a priest and a libertine?"

Pickett rolled her eyes. "Fine. What?"

"A strong drink."

A thousand versions of that joke had been told a thousand times, each by someone thinking they were a comic genius. And yet, coming from Edie, in her worn-out shoes with her pleasant smile, it somehow didn't make Pickett grimace. Not that she'd dare laugh either. The situation was too dire and the joke was too awful.

"Maybe we should put *you* on stage," Pickett said, shaking her head. "Telling rotten jokes and giving the audience a dance. You're a good dancer, aren't you?"

"Not the sort to dance by herself on a stage without music." Edie swung her legs back and forth, back and forth, the shadows of her feet skimming over the gray water. She tucked a yellow lock of hair behind her ear and glanced sidelong at Pickett. "So dead things are rising out of the swamp then."

"Looks like."

Edie went very still. Then, all too casually, pulled her feet up onto the boardwalk. "Any idea how?"

"If I did, you think I'd have dumped the fish?" Pickett sighed and leaned back against the half-rotted planks, staring up at the night sky. Through the clouds, she could see the stars, but she couldn't make out any constellations. It seemed the gods were not inclined to grant her an omen. Then again, even if they did, she'd be the least likely candidate to interpret them properly.

Edie lay back next to her, her hands folded over her stomach. "I think we might be in trouble."

"How could a witch be in trouble in her own domain?" Pickett asked sullenly.

Edie snorted but continued on as though she hadn't heard a word. "Dead things are rising up out of the water, so far a fish and a frog. Hopefully just fish and frogs but even that could be bad." She began picking at her lip–a habit Pickett had come to recognize as a sign that Edie was worry-thinking. She'd be complaining about the taste of blood for days, but she did it to herself. If this kept up, though, Edie's head was going to do far worse to her.

Pickett swatted Edie's arm, then grabbed her hand, pinning it to the boardwalk between them. Edie just moved on to worrying her lip with her teeth, which was arguably less damaging.

"All right," Edie muttered. "Dead things rising up. And living things pulled from the swamp are definitely making people sick. Those swamp crabs were good quality."

"That's seriously what you're worried about?"

Edie wrinkled her nose. "I'm a very good cook. My stew should have been perfect."

"And now people will warn others not to eat at the Pick's Pocket." Pickett sighed and draped an arm over her face. "Edie, we had to give away so much money."

"Refunds aren't the same as giving away."

"They are when they impact my profits."

Edie swatted Pickett's arm. "Priorities, Pickett."

Pickett dropped her arm to glare at her. "You try running a business then you come complaining to me about priorities."

"You run a con, Pickett."

"Business, con, priest, libertine. It's all a matter of inebriation."

"Suppose you're all of those things wrapped in a colorful cape." Edie leaned over her, yellow hair falling into her face. The moon shone like a crown behind her head, casting her in an odd, godly sort of light. It made Pickett feel like a waterbug in a wave. It made her feel like the most important thing in the world. It made her feel like, if she ever decided to settle down and learn enough about the gods to worship one, she'd probably pick one who looked like Edie.

A long moment passed, and it dawned on Pickett that, maybe, just maybe, Edie didn't have any words to say. Neither did Pickett. They looked at each other eye to eye, truly allowing the depth and richness of their situation to simmer between them. Edie was a foundling milkmaid, mistrusted by her village, who'd escaped to the swamp seeking safety. Pickett was a con-woman, less clever and more charming enough to convince everyone she was clever and powerful when even she knew she wasn't.

They both depended on this rotting shack to protect them. But the one man Pickett needed to charm above all others could not be charmed. And the very swamps that surrounded them had turned vile and poisoned. How long until the traders decided they didn't want to waste time stopping into the bar? How long until they decided to bypass the swamp altogether? How long until Pickett and Edie were once more two women flung out into the world, desperate to find a way to survive until old age?

She sighed and patted Edie's cheek.

"I suppose you think we ought to get to the bottom of what's going on in the swamp?"

Edie swallowed, then nodded. "As much as I appreciate you admitting I was right, I don't get to gloat."

"There's always time to gloat."

Edie smiled sadly. "Then maybe the situation sucked the joy out of it. We're the only business out here, and folks think you're a swamp witch. Sooner or later, they're going to catch on. And they'll want answers."

Oh yes. And Pickett knew all too well what small-minded Sedrian folk did when they wanted answers. Edie knew too, or she'd never have fled to the swamp for safety.

"I'm the witch. Not you. You're not responsible for answers."

Edie's expression twisted into something sharp and unpleasant. Something that didn't suit her otherwise gentle nature.

"This is my home."

Pickett's heart swelled up. Home. This bar, with its holes in the floor and its lousy drinks, was a home. Pickett's home. Edie's home. *Their* home. Letting herself think it was like grabbing for a peach growing in a meja's garden. Sweet and worthwhile for only a moment, before the consequences followed.

She shouldn't let herself get attached. If Edie belonged to the bar, then she belonged to its troubles. Pickett would just drag her down. Someone as good and kind as Edie didn't deserve that. Just thinking it made her heart shrivel up to its usual size.

"Edie—"

"This is my *home*," she hissed. "You let me in. You let me make this my home. I keep telling you and you refuse to listen, but I deserve to be a part of protecting it or else I'm just some helpless waif who's at someone else's mercy. Again!"

In that moment, Edie looked like a glass shark, ready to rip its enemy to shreds. It was so jarring against the pretty bodice and the memory of her gentle smiles. Still. It suited her just as well. If she found out the truth of just how fragile everything was, she'd fight for it. Throw herself into it with everything she had. Edie'd march up to Fistic and demand a better deal, forever linking her name to Pickett's debt. Worse than that, people might start asking questions. They'd wonder how Edie came to work at the bar. They'd find out she'd come from Gallraven. They'd look into why she'd run away from that village and what happened to the man who'd chased her right up to Pickett's door.

Better not to give her the option. If the bar went under and dragged Pickett with it, Edie would be free to walk away. She'd be angry. She'd feel betrayed. But Edie, at least, would be all right.

The thought cheered Pickett a little. Even if everything went belly-up, she'd make sure Edie could get out. Pickett grinned.

"You, Edie, are at nobody's mercy." Pickett pushed herself up on her hands, the old wood of the boardwalk creaking underneath, and stopped within just a few inches of Edie's nose. "I'm nothing if not difficult. But I've never been one to give up."

"How?" Edie hissed, giving Pickett's shoulder a shove. "How are you going to not give up on this place?"

Pickett glanced around. She couldn't magically conjure entertainment. That had been a bust. Then again, she'd found Ovlovey performing at a festival in a small village a month ago. Maybe her luck would win out again. And, this time, maybe the good luck would last longer than the bad.

"Research," she offered. "I'll keep going into any town with a library open to the likes of me. See what I can learn. Maybe it'll be enough to keep us open a little longer."

Maybe Edie could see the lie of omission. Maybe she couldn't. Maybe she was foolish. Maybe she was kind. Either way, it didn't much matter. Edie scowled and leaned back on her heels.

"Fine," she said. "Just swear to me you aren't giving up on this place."

"Not until the planks rot out beneath us," Pickett promised. "Now. I'm hungry. Anything to eat?"

"Sure. But the bread's a couple days old and the cheese has gone a little blue."

Pickett wrinkled her nose. "Really? Is that all?"

At last, Edie pulled away and shrugged. "Well. There was swamp crab stew, but I doubt you want that.

WITHOUT THE ABILITY TO live off the fat of the swamp, they had to make do with what was already in the larder, which meant hard tack. Fortunately, Edie was the enterprising sort who could turn a pile of old carrots and sprouting onions into a passable spread, but her efforts were met with unhappy grunts.

"What happened to the fish?" Slurne asked sullenly, dunking his bread into a flagon of beer a few times before taking a small, resentful nibble.

"He moved on to bigger and better things," Pickett told him. "Show business is an ever-changing industry."

Slurne grunted, tapping the tack against the table as sailors often did to knock the weevils out. Interesting. He didn't strike her as the sort to have long sea experience.

"This tack's hard as a rock," he muttered.

"Easier on the stomach than the stew, I assure you." Pickett glanced around. A couple of traders had come and gone without purchasing a single drink. Slurne's friend, Arn, remained a no-show. Even the Northfellow hadn't taken up his usual place at the bar. The stage sat conspicuously empty. What would Fistic's "friend" think when he inevitably came out to check on the place? Would Fistic decide it was time to close out this particular loan?

If he did, he'd lose money. Pickett shivered at the thought of how he might go about trying to get that money back. Indentured servants didn't exactly have rights in Sedrios, and she'd heard that those who had substantial debts were sent out to plantations or dropped onto pirate-hunting vessels—as good as guaranteed death. How long would her debts force her to serve? A year? Two? Surely the crumbling old bar wouldn't be worth more than three.

She glanced sidelong at Edie, who didn't let her tight, forced smile slip a hair. And yet Pickett spotted her tugging at a thread in her skirt. Edie couldn't pay the price. If it came to that, then Pickett could pretend she didn't know her. She'd never seen her. Edie wasn't even an employee. Just some patron who really liked to drink here. No reason both their lives should be destroyed.

Pickett took a steadying breath and fought to remind herself that this was a good thing. If the bar failed and she was indentured to pay off her debt, Edie would get out. If she squinted and had a lot to drink, Pickett could probably convince herself that was enough of a win.

Slurne grunted and took a long pull of his beer before belching into his fist. "This place is deader than that fish. At least he had some energy."

"What're you gonna do, go drink at any of the other establishments in the swamp?"

"I might," he sniffed. "If anyone else is crazy enough to open one."

Pickett scowled. "Shut up and eat your rock."

After Slurne left, there were no other customers. There likely wouldn't be. Even the Northfellow hadn't bothered to show up. After the disastrous swamp crab stew and the lack of any other draw, their only hope would be a rainy night to drive travelers indoors. And rain would bring with it fresh leaks, fresh repairs, fresh drains on the already meager savings in the lockbox.

She needed to do something about this mess or they'd starve to death inside of a slowly rotting shack. Assuming Fistic didn't evict them the second she failed to make the early payment.

After their pitiful evening, even Edie had struggled to maintain a chipper attitude as she trudged off to the back room where their respective cots had been made. Pickett waited until that pretty face began unleashing loud, toad-like snores before she grabbed her cape and slipped out.

The Sedrian swamps were well-traveled, what with people taking the boardwalks from town to town, trading, fishing, and the like. But few to no people ever actually tried to settle in the murky waters. Not when it was possible to follow the wooden slats to the next safe spot.

Pickett knew she was crazy enough to do it. But there was one other person who was actually crazier than her. Maybe crazier was what she needed. Maybe he'd have fresh insight on this whole rotten situation. At this point, Pickett would talk to a goat's ass if she thought the answer might be in one of its farts.

Hoag's boat floated where it always did, right at the intersection of two walkways, moored by a heavy rope thick with mildew. The boat itself was blocky, like someone had fitted an actual house on top of a large and sturdy boat and declared it done. Not good for much more than floating, honestly, which made Pickett wonder why Hoag didn't just live in a proper shack. It'd bob less. Of course, the answer was as clear as anything.

If Pickett was crazy for living in the swamp, Hoag was a lunatic.

Lashed to the boardwalk was a long staff. Pickett untied it, then leaned out, stretching her arm and the staff to bang thrice on the door. There came the sound of pans clattering before the door flung open and Hoag popped his head out. His patchy, thinning red hair stuck out in all directions. Mixed with the particular pale shade of his brown skin, it made him look rather like a torch about to go out. His eyes darted left, then right, before settling on her. There was something unnerving about those eyes. They shone like he had just discovered buried treasure at all times, regardless of the circumstances. She didn't know his past, but from what she'd been able to piece together, this was what happened when regular people came in touch with the wrong sort of magics. The brain just couldn't withstand it.

"Business?" he asked gruffly, in the clipped tone of a former military man.

Pickett set the staff back down and flung out her cape before giving a salute. "Yes, sir. Information, sir."

Hoag watched the flutter of the cape. He liked it when she flared it out. A wide grin spread across his face, showing his missing canine before he dipped his head several times, gesturing her to follow him. She did, stepping onto the wobbly boat.

Inside the house, it smelled like mold and was about as easy to find a place to sit as it was to find gold up a fishmonger's asshole. She picked for a moment through the flotsam and jetsam of Hoag's home—empty bottles, fish hooks, tattered nets, colorful pots filled with beads and stones, and, this time, a rough wooden carving of an anatomically inaccurate squid. Who even knew how long that would be there?

Eventually, she found an upturned bucket and sank down onto it. Hoag dug around through his chaos for a bit but, instead of handing her a drink or a snack, he dropped a stuffed rabbit into her lap. Pickett stroked its linen ears sagely as he finally settled in the stack of old pillows and cloth that made up his bed.

"So. What brings the mighty swamp witch to my realm?" Hoag asked somberly. "Have you seen a vision of my demise?"

"Believe it or not, I actually need some help."

He threw back his head and laughed like a seal. "Help a witch?"

"Even we powerful wielders of magic can have blind spots, Hoag. And you know the swamp in ways I do not."

Hoag snapped back into a serious, dour expression. "I see. Are we all going to die?"

"What? No, I mean, I don't think so." Pickett shook her head. "But there's something wrong with the creatures in the swamp. They're behaving strangely and they're no longer good to eat. Bad for business. And"—she waved one hand, careful to keep the other atop the linen bunny—"bad for nature and the balance of all magics and life and bitey bugs and the like."

"The creatures?" Hoag wrinkled his nose and tugged at his thin, red hair. "No, no I do not think. Hrm."

He reached behind him, pulling out a long ladle, bigger than any Pickett had ever seen. She schooled her expression into a carefully neutral one. It wouldn't do for Hoag to wonder why the "witch" was surprised by anything.

He scrambled off the bed, kicked aside some old boots and a box that jingled with the sounds of broken glass, and revealed a large trap door in the floor. He opened it, lowering the ladle down, down, down. Then he froze, brows furrowed, eyes shining as he gazed through the hatch.

Pickett fidgeted in her seat, tugging on the ears of the bunny as she glanced around. She sort of wished Hoag had offered her a snack instead of a toy. The hard tack hadn't exactly made for a satisfying meal.

At long last, he pulled the ladle up, up, up, its bowl filled with the murky, brown water of the swamp, unfiltered and unboiled. Without a moment's hesitation, he drank from it, water and mud and algae and fish shit and all.

The hard tack threatened to reappear. Pickett had to bite her cheek to keep it down.

Hoag smacked his lips and nodded. "Thought I tasted it but didn't think to investigate further."

"Well?" Pickett urged.

Hoag closed the trap door, retreating to his bed, holding the ladle like a child. "It's not the creatures; it's the waters," he said sadly, and he began to rock back and forth. "Not harmful for us. Not for the land creatures. But the swamp creatures? They live in the water. They breathe it. It's in their very skin. They're sick with it."

Sick with it. Pickett thought back to Letterboy nursing his finger. If there was something in the water getting into the fish . . .

"If someone gets bit by one of these things, what do you think happens?"

Hoag wiggled his fingers over his chest. "The afflicted portion will be as affected as the water. No flushing it out of the flesh while it's in the water. The wound will remain as long as the waters are rancid with this curse."

Yeah. Letterboy was definitely going to lose that finger. Pickett wrinkled her nose. "So the water is poisoned?"

"In a way," Hoag said. "Poisoned with hope and heartbreak."

"Right, so is that some new powder they're selling in Southfen or—"

"Hope and heartbreak." Hoag scowled and poked her arm

with the ladle. "Sorrow has poisoned our swamp. As our witch, you are the only one who can heal us all."

"Right." Pickett smacked the ladle out of the way with the stuffed bunny. "And how do I do that?"

Hoag shrugged. "No idea."

Great. Pickett rose and sank into a deep bow, offering another little cape flourish. "Thank you for the wisdom, Hoag. As always, it was adventurous."

She set the stuffed bunny back on the pile of junk and made to leave when Hoag scrambled out of his seat. "Wait! Wait, my witch." He snagged the anatomically inaccurate squid off the pile and held it out to her. "I beg your blessing for my new friend."

Pickett blinked. "You know it's a wooden statue, right?"

Hoag nodded and pulled a gleaming coin from his pocket. Pickett didn't hesitate to rest one hand on the wooden shaft of the squid, inclining her head.

"May your forested origins not keep from you the blessings of the sea," she said. "Though you'll have to take the boardwalk to Southfen to see it."

"Boardwalk to Southfen," Hoag said, his eyes shining just a little brighter, this time with unshed tears.

For good measure, Pickett even dropped a little kiss onto the wooden statue.

When she returned to the Pick's Pocket just before dawn, it was with a freshly purchased bag of potatoes and a block of cheese. Enough to keep them afloat one more night.

NINE

Once more, the Pick's Pocket filled with the smell of cooking food. Hard tack, yes. But also roasting potatoes. It was bound to sell a great deal better than the hard tack, and even if it didn't, Pickett would eat well that night.

The only problem was getting people in the door.

In order to keep what Edie referred to as "the magic stink" from interfering with her cooking, Pickett went outside to mix her tricks. Admittedly, the black powder did have a bit of an acrid smell to it, but it was no worse than the muddy swamp. Pickett settled down by the back door, pausing to ensure there was no risk of a new undead fish flopping up beside her, then got to work. As she combined the powders and colors, she glanced periodically down into the gray swamp waters. Hoag had said the waters were like this, because they were full of heartbreak. So the Rottering swamp was sad? Why was it sad? Maybe it was because people like her kept insulting it.

Well, she knew what usually cheered people up.

She cleared her throat. "Um, you're looking particularly muddy today, swamp."

The waters rippled as a swamp crab moved under the surface.

"Is that some new swamp grass you're sprouting? Cause it's working for you."

Pickett carefully began to mix the powders together, too slow for the powders to do whatever it was they did when she went too fast. If only it were so easy to fix things and make the water happy again. But it didn't hurt to try. That certainly beat laying down and accepting that her business was going to dry up and die like a bug in the sun.

"Listen," she said, "between us, I'm in some trouble. I can't lose my bar. I can't. I've got nothing else. Edie's got nothing else. And maybe I get sent away to work off my debt, and she's all alone." She leaned forward, glaring at the water. "I get if you don't want to help me out. I'm an asshole. But get your act together for—" The door to the Pick's Pocket flew open.

"Pickett." Edie hissed.

Pickett jerked, and the powder in her hand exploded with a loud *bang!*

Her cheeks stung. The smell of burning hair filled the air, and Pickett only just managed to pat her unruly curls to ensure they weren't still on fire. She gave a little cough, expelling a soft, gray puff, and wiped some of the acrid ash from her face.

"Edie." She growled, but Edie wasn't cowed.

Edie ducked down next to Pickett, her eyes wide as she fiddled with the rough handle of one of their kitchen knives. "There's a man inside."

Pickett blinked. "Then serve him? We're a bar, Edie."

But Edie pulled a face. "He makes my teeth bite."

"What the hell does that mean?"

"My teeth bite. It's what people say in Gallraven. It means . . ." Edie bit her lip and glanced up at the sky. "It means . . ."

"I get it. I get it." Pickett smeared some of the mess off her face, poured the remaining powder into a bag, and tucked that bag into one of her many pockets. With a small shake of her shoulders, she pulled on her witch persona. A bartender, yes. But also a threat in case he meant any harm to Edie. "You hold down the kitchen. I'll serve your teeth-biter."

Edie shot her a relieved smile before she scurried back inside. Pickett didn't bother trying to clean up further. Sometimes, the evidence of an explosion added mystique to the mad-swamp-witch act.

The fellow sitting at the bar was not one of their regulars. Even strangers from afar occasionally wandered the swamps, after all. He also didn't seem to have a similar occupation to the sorts she usually served. His thick, canvas breeches and coat were tough and sturdy, good for travel but not for fishing or farming. It was clearly good quality, but not what she'd come to expect of a merchant. Those sorts usually wore fine waistcoats and the like to show off some degree of wealth and, therefore, success. Nor did he have the oversized bag typical of a tinker or trader. It was just him sitting at the bar in a canvas coat and a wide-brimmed hat. The edge of something wooden stuck out from his jacket, and Pickett knew the shape of a crossbow when she saw it. Not very subtle of him.

He wasn't what she'd expected Fistic's "friend" to look like, but here he was.

Pickett clenched her jaw. Now it made sense. Teeth biter.

She managed to twist her face into something of a sharp smile, or she at least hoped it was a smile, before she sidled up behind the bar and snatched a freshly washed glass.

"So what brings you out here, stranger?" she asked.

The man grunted and scratched his salt-and-pepper beard. "Passing through."

Passing through her freckled bottom. Pickett reached for the pitcher of bibblewood juice, measuring out a smaller-than-usual pour of it before she added the rum—a bit more of that than usual. "Well, good thing you dropped in. We look to be a haven for travelers of the Rottering swamp."

The man grunted and turned, glancing around. "Doesn't look like you're busy." He observed. "How is it you can afford to stay open?"

Ice trickled down Pickett's smile. She squeezed the glass before slowly, intentionally, sliding it across the bar. So Fistic really wasn't trusting her to make enough money to stay open. Smart for him. Bad for her. How the hell was she supposed to convince someone things were fine when he was the only one sitting at her bar?

"Most of our travelers happen by in the evenings. That's when we offer food," Pickett said tartly. "Will you be staying that long, stranger?"

"I may. Could be good to get a glimpse at the regulars."

The regulars being Slurne and one or two others. No, no, no. If this guy had been sent to poke around into how the bar was doing, then the last thing Pickett needed him to see was an empty bar both day and night.

But how could she get him to keep away?

The stranger lifted the glass to his lips and . . . shit. Pickett only just saw the crack in it. This was not looking good. Would he report just how decrepit the place was to his boss? Would Fistic even care? Or would Fistic see it as further proof that closing in on the bar was the smart financial option?

Before he could take a sip, she gasped, slapping a hand to her head and stumbling back. She made certain to fling out her cape, just for added effect.

The stranger blinked and lowered his glass.

"Uh, miss? You all right?"

Pickett let out a low moan, swaying back and forth, rolling her eyes back the way she'd learned when one of the Dames wanted to frighten away an unsavory customer. She held it until her eyes began to ache and she heard the telltale shift of an ass in a seat, signaling that she had officially made the stranger uncomfortable, before she snapped back hard enough for her hair to flop forward, briefly obscuring her view. When she pushed it back, she saw the stranger staring at her warily, like she'd had some sort of magical fit.

Good.

She lurched forward, pretending to shake off the vestiges of a fit, and grabbed his hand. Before he could yank back, she flipped it over and started running her fingers over all the lines, calluses, and even a scar at the heel of his palm. Definitely not the hand of someone typically sent around to talk to people.

"Oh goodness." Pickett breathed. "Oh goodness me, sir. The fates have not been kind to you."

"I dunno about that." The man quirked a brow and reached for his drink again, but Pickett slapped his palm hard.

"You were sent to me today, so I could warn you away!"

He sighed, setting the glass down so he could lean forward. "Fine. I'll bite. Warn me away from what?"

From what indeed? Pickett ran her fingers over his palm again while snatching the glass away and tucking it neatly out of sight. In hindsight, it might have been wise to learn how fortune tellers actually did this before trying to mimic one, but desperate times and all that.

"You're seeking something." She tilted her head one way, then another, daring to steal a glance at his face before she grunted to herself. He was giving her nothing, the bastard.

"As a matter of fact, I am."

Oh? Pickett glanced up, balanced in that moment when she didn't know if she was saved or fucked.

The man pulled his hand back and leaned forward, his expression dark. "You get folk from all the villages around here?"

"Many of them, yes."

"You ever get folk from Gallraven?"

And just like that, they'd tipped into fucked. Pickett had to stop herself from glancing over her shoulder at the kitchen where Edie was cooking up a storm. Instead, she busied herself with selecting another glass, the nicest one she had, and making him a fresh drink.

"That town doesn't tend to send people out and about," Pickett said carefully.

"It's only an hour out by foot."

"True, but they're a superstitious folk," Pickett pointed out, heart jumping from her gut to her throat. "They don't come out here much."

"Well, that's why I've come. Missing person."

Fucking fuckfish. This was worse than the guy being sent by Fistic. He couldn't be law enforcement. Could he? No of course not. Edie would have recognized him if he was actually from her shitty little village. More than that, he'd have recognized her and the crime Pickett could only assume Gallraven suspected Edie had committed. If he didn't recognize her, he didn't know. If he didn't know, Edie must be safe. He must be a bounty hunter, which hopefully meant Pickett could direct him elsewhere.

It was fine. Everything was fine. She just had to push him away, and everything would be fine.

And nobody would find Marnoc's body unless they felt like taking a dip in the swamp under the bar. But even a blind dog can sniff out a bone. Pickett needed him gone. Fast.

"Oooh." Pickett moaned, swaying back and forth before steadying herself on the counter. "That's what fate was whispering to me. Gallraven. Yes. Seeking someone from Gallraven. That's why the fates have been very bad for you."

"Just a job, ma'am," the stranger said, lifting his glass again.

"A job you will regret," Pickett said gloomily as she pushed the fresh glass toward him. "My advice? Drop it. Get on a ship. Sail to the Paradisals. Get rich hunting down deserting sailors in the islands. Nothing good awaits the end of a job from Gallraven."

He snorted and lifted the glass to his lips, then spat it out, spraying rum and spit and bibblewood juice all over her nice semi-clean counter.

"Eyugh! What is that?" He wiped his lips on his sleeve.

"Bibblewood and rum. A specialty." Pickett grinned wickedly. "It's that or beer."

"Keep 'em both." He slammed a couple of shims down onto the counter without bothering to ask if that was how much he owed and rose, striding out. Pickett narrowed her eyes, grabbing the glass to empty it herself.

Something told her that, for all her efforts, he hadn't been scared away yet.

TEN

That night, as they both climbed up into the loft bedroom just above the bar, Pickett tried very hard not to notice the knife Edie brought up with her. Of course, it was hard to do that when Edie didn't even attempt to swing at subtlety. She kept it within hand's reach all throughout changing for bed and even tucked it under her pillow like some magic talisman.

Pickett could try to keep her safe, but in the end this bar might be more danger to Edie than anything else. If Fistic didn't find out about her and decide to try and wring some of the debt out of her too, then bounty hunters might drag her back to that shitty little village. Pickett didn't know what Gallraven did to killer milkmaids. The fact that it was the sort of place that produced the maniac who'd chased her into the swamp in the first place, Pickett didn't suspect it could be anything good.

She cleared her throat.

"Listen, Edie," she said softly. "Maybe it would be a good idea for you to pack a bag. In case that hunter shows up again, I mean. Just a quick way to sneak out the back."

"What?" Edie shot right up, her eyes so wide that, even in the poor lantern light of their room, Pickett could see the whites all around her eyes.

"Just a precaution," Pickett hurried to say, but it was too late. The damage was done.

Edie fiddled with her nightgown, working an existing hole steadily larger.

"He knows about Marnoc doesn't he? Someone sent him to find Marnoc's killer. Someone connected it to me and they know I'm here and—"

"Hey, hey, hey." Pickett scooted forward, grabbing Edie's wrists before she could rip into the hole any further. "We can barely afford to keep this place open. I can't go buying you a new nightgown. Deep breaths."

Edie did not take a deep breath. As far as Pickett could tell, she didn't even take a shallow breath.

"Someone is going to come for me. What if Marnoc rose from the swamp? He could have gone home. He could have told them that I killed him."

"Only after he tried to kill you first." Pickett shifted, forcing Edie to meet her eyes as she squeezed her hands. "Listen to me. Nobody is going to take you away. Do you really think Marnoc's tongue wouldn't have rotted out by now?"

"But—"

"No." Pickett pressed a finger to Edie's lips. "Nobody outside of your shitty village knows who you are or what you look like. Even if they hired someone, which they definitely didn't, nobody would know to find you here, because they definitely won't cross the swamp witch. If anything, they'll assume I killed him for trespassing."

It wasn't entirely a lie. Sure, it was enough of one to make her insides churn, but it was a lie of protection. If Edie panicked, Edie might make mistakes. She couldn't know about Fistic or she might fight to protect the bar. She might put herself in his path. She might get herself indentured along with Pickett. She couldn't believe the bounty hunter was a threat or she might reveal herself. Edie might even try to fight him if it came to it. Pickett had watched this sweet milk-turned-kitchen maid beat a dangerous man over the head with a chair then dump his bound body into the swamp while he was still conscious. She could make impulsive decisions. At a time like this, impulsive was the last thing they needed.

Edie batted Pickett's hand aside.

"Then that'll endanger you, won't it? As far as they know, the night I disappeared, so did he. If they figured out he died in the swamp and connect it to you—"

"It's why I cultivated the swamp witch image in the first place. Nobody fucks with a mysterious witch. Especially not the only one around who'll sell them beer and rum."

Edie sighed. "Right. You're the swamp witch. But they have no reason to fear me."

"They fear me enough for the both of us," Pickett assured her. "Edie, what happened that night never needs to happen again. I won't let you land in a position where you ever have to kill anyone ever again."

It wasn't much but it was at least what Pickett could promise. At least to the best of her ability.

Edie gave her a queasy smile. "I appreciate it, but can you really promise something like that?"

"Why wouldn't I?"

Edie's lips thinned. "Because, Pickett. The dead are rising from the swamp and, tongue or no, Marnoc is one of the dead within the swamp. I doubt whatever's happening will end with fish and frogs."

"Then we'll defend our home. And I'll defend you," Pickett promised. How she'd do it, she still didn't know.

Edie just nodded absently and pulled away to blow out the candle with a quick puff. Pickett climbed down the stairs to take her watch. For the whole of the night, she couldn't help watching for specters she could only hope would never rise.

CHAPTER

ELEVEN

If there was one thing Pickett could rely on, it was the power of a good show. Despite any previous complaints about the smell of working with these particular powders inside, she wasn't about to leave the bar alone again, just in case the hunter returned. When she was done mixing everything up, she rolled out some thin clay, tamping everything down before she rolled it all around a short cord. She repeated this over and over again until she had a dozen clay balls drying in the windowsill.

When dusk finally came, Pickett gathered her little explosives and headed out to the dock. It was a waste of resources, really. But if she couldn't get some customers in, there was nothing else to use them for. One by one, Pickett lit the wick on each of the clay balls before tossing them in the air to explode in a shower of light and color and charred, dusty bits of clay. Each time, she imagined a different person's face bursting above her.

Romona Ovlovey.

BAM!

Fistic.

BAM!

The bounty hunter.

BAM!

The monster who'd chased Edie into the swamp. Every person who'd ever hurt her. Even the rotten fish, wherever it was now. The thoughts of their brains splattered in the sky was soothing, if only for a moment.

When she spied the first traveler heading her way, Pickett ducked back into the bar. Edie stood behind the counter, brandishing a fresh plate of, well, Pickett didn't really know what she was looking at but it looked fucking amazing. Each potato had been sliced over and over without being cut all the way through, and each slice held a melted gob of cheese and salt and a little bit of hot, red spice.

"I call them tater shims," Edie said proudly. "They were easier than a lot of things and since you buy a whole potato, I figured we could charge a half pip each."

Pickett breathed in the rich, cheesy, earthy smell and snagged one. Any fear she might have had that people would be afraid to eat with them again fled her mind as the flavor exploded on her tongue.

"Mm," she hummed. "Best make it a whole pip."

"We might not sell out."

Pickett peeled one of the slices free, pulling a long string of cheese with it. If it meant they could save a couple for themselves, it was a sacrifice she was willing to make. It was certainly the best they'd eaten in a while.

"Make it a whole," Pickett repeated.

Edie shrugged and reached over to rip a cheesy slice from Pickett's tater shim. She shoved it into her mouth with a little hum, leaving a sheen of grease on her lips.

"With how you talk about money, I wouldn't have expected you to come back with these ingredients." Edie mused, but her blue eyes were sharp as she looked Pickett up and down.

Did Pickett dare tell Edie about Hoag and his advice? About

Fistic? With the way things were going, it was starting to feel worse and worse to hide this from Edie. But how did she crawl out of the hole without looking like a complete ass in front of the one person who looked at her like she wasn't one?

Pickett teetered for a moment, then backed up and gave Edie a roguish smirk. Edie scowled, but just then the door opened and the first trader wandered in, surveying them with suspicion. At least until he spied the tater shims.

Soon enough, Pickett found herself sitting on the stage, doing exactly what she'd sworn she never would—magic tricks.

With every bit of deception she could muster, Pickett flicked her wrists, hiding the flints on her fingers and the little clay smoke bombs up her sleeve as she filled the air with colorful sparks, earning appreciative hums from what few patrons she had.

Bloody waste of expensive materials. It didn't get half the gawks the foul dead fish had gotten. Pickett glanced at the chair at the corner of the bar and found it empty. Even the North-fellow wasn't here. She couldn't remember the last time he'd failed to show up for his nightly beer. Was he embarrassed about his maudlin behavior the last time they spoke? Hopefully that was it. She shuddered to think of what could happen to a barmy old drunk in this swamp.

Slurne, at least, seemed to be enjoying himself. Strange. He'd been back almost every night, and without the company of his friend Arn once again. He didn't even bother clambering behind the corner table to take a spot playing dice. He knocked back two glasses of bibblewood rum, then carried another along with a tater shim up to the stage, plopping down, looking like a sail that had lost its wind.

Pickett brushed some of the ash off onto her trouser leg.

"Slurne," she said.

"Witch," he muttered, taking a hearty bite of the potato,

then a glug of bibblewood rum. He hiccupped, then sighed. "Wish you'd have done this sooner. Arn would've loved it."

"I expect he would. Where is your smarmy friend, anyway."

"Dunno. Not at home. His missus threw a pot at my head. I was in my pints at the time so I didn't properly catch what she yelled, but I got the gist of it." He snorted, his hefty mustache trembling under his breath. "She blamed me for him being gone. Seems to think I dragged him into a life of debauchery."

"Yes, like you'd have to drag a dog to a chicken dinner." But something didn't feel right. "So neither you nor his wife have seen him?"

Slurne shook his head sadly. "No. You don't suppose something happened? It's only that I grew up hearing there was no swamp witch, and here you are. So when people tell me there's no swamp beast . . ." He furrowed his brows. "Arn was pretty drunk the last time I saw him. He might have fallen. You don't think . . ."

Pickett hummed noncommittally as the door opened, but it wasn't the bounty hunter. Just a tall man with a moustache like a comb. He sniffed and turned, heading straight for the bar.

She leaned over, trying to catch Edie's eye, but Edie was deep in conversation with a woman who looked to be some sort of tinker, judging by her massive bag. She didn't seem to be stressed or unhappy, so that was something good.

The moustache man straightened his waistcoat before sitting in the Northfellow's seat. Pickett narrowed her eyes. Hard to say what was more upsetting: that the man was wearing a nice waistcoat in a place like this or that the Northfellow wasn't currently in that seat.

"What's worse is the fish are biting something fierce out in those waters." Slurne lamented with a loud, trumpeting sniffle. "You can see it clear as a fucking . . . clear shit. The waters are alive with movement. Arn would have brought home buckets full of fish without ever having to try at all. Unless they got him first."

"Uh huh." Pickett leaned forward, narrowing her eyes. The man in the fine waistcoat was leaning forward, speaking to Edie, who had gone stone still. He wore a pewter ring on his middle finger, and Pickett didn't have to see it up close to know the insignia it would bear—three coins above a schooner. Fuck. This had to be Fistic's enforcer.

Was he telling Edie about Fistic? About the debt? Was he threatening her? Pickett leaned forward, neck stiffening as she scowled. Slurne babbled on.

Pickett's hand shot forward, squeezing Slurne's arm. "Hey, maybe someone else has seen him."

"Huh?" Slurne blinked, his eyes glazed over with drink and emotion.

"As far as we know, no regular here knows where Arn is. But"—she raised her brows and jerked her chin toward the bar —"there's a new guy here. What a coincidence that he shows up when Arn has gone missing."

"Right. Coincidence." Slurne's brows furrowed, his eyes darting back and forth as he peered closely at her.

Pickett sighed and planted her hand on his head, swiveling it until he could see the stranger. "Maybe he has something to do with your friend disappearing on you."

Slurne grunted before lumbering forward in a rum-soaked haze. Pickett might feel worse about unleashing him on the enforcer if Slurne had, himself, been a better person. Pickett half watched as she tugged a fresh, tiny pack of black powder from her sleeve, slipping it between her fingers as she slicked her flintstone rings. Blue fire burst from her hand. Appreciative applause was followed by a few pips and shims tossed onto the stage. Slurne approached the enforcer, letting out a soft belch before wagging a finger in the man's face.

Edie began inching away. Pickett allowed herself a second to relax.

At least until the enforcer's bristle-brush moustache curled and he drew back, his strong fingers curling into a hammer of a fist. Pickett leaped off the stage, but she was too late. That fist collided with Slurne's face, sending the old trader to the ground in a splash of rum.

Oh good fuck.

Pickett raced over to Slurne before he passed out right there. She didn't like the man, but if he puked while he was unconscious, he'd choke on it. This place didn't need more death than it already had. All the while, Edie shouted at the man, who shouted back at her.

"Every last shim! Them's me orders. Every last shim comes with me tonight!"

"We're not in the business of being shaken down by thugs," Edie snapped, and Pickett couldn't overlook the way Edie was backing up, reaching for the broom leaning against the wall behind her.

"I see you've come early, sir," Pickett said, trying her best to make her voice drip with honey, the way successful business owners could. She gestured to Edie. "Have you had our specialty? We add bibblewood juice to the rum. It gives a nice—"

"I'm not here to drink." He growled.

Pickett gestured around her. "You're in a bar. Serving people is what we do."

"I am in Mr. Fistic's bar and I have come to collect Mr. Fistic's money."

Pickett bunched her hands into fists, her expression hardening. Edie stared at her with wide, bright eyes. Her lovely mouth twisted into a dark scowl.

Shit. Shitwater and the bastards that defecated in it.

"What didn't you tell me?" Edie asked, her words soft

enough for only Pickett and the enforcer to hear. But she might as well have shouted it for all that the words rang in Pickett's ears.

Pickett swallowed, glancing around her. Every eye in the bar was on them. On her. On the so-called sorceress and the intruder into her establishment. Fistic would have sent someone who wouldn't be scared off by tricks. But she had to try.

"I advise you have a drink and a seat," Pickett said, flicking her wrist and . . . *Oh no*. She flicked her wrist again but no black powder pack settled into her palm.

"If I return without a bag of coin, Fistic'll have me balls."

"And you're more scared of him than a witch?" Edie snarled.

The enforcer didn't even glance up at her. He just kept staring at Pickett his lips twitching in and out of a smile.

"Go on then, witch." He growled, his breath stinking of old sausage. "Do something. Prove you're something scary."

Every eye was on her, waiting for her to do something. And Pickett didn't know what she could do. Knee him in the balls? A guy like this might just be able to take it and knock her out. Give him the money and prove she couldn't protect this place?

She opened her mouth, not quite sure what was going to come out, when the door quite literally flew open. Splinters of wood rained through the air as the rickety, half-rotted old thing crashed to the ground. And behind it stood Arn. His shoulders slumped forward. One eye bulged, almost out of the socket. His head lolled to the side, unsupported by the huge chunk ripped from one side of his neck, right to the bone.

Well, she'd be fucked twice on a Dagoday. Maybe there was such a thing as a swamp beast after all. And Arn had come back to show off his wounds.

CHAPTER
TWELVE

Arn the fisherman was as alive as a eunuch's balls, but there he stood with half his throat ripped out, swaying on half-rotted legs. Pale flesh bubbled out from the gaps and rips in his clothes, no doubt adding to the putrid stink of him. If Pickett had to bet on it, she'd say he'd had a couple of days to rot in the waters before he bounced back to whatever non-life he suddenly experienced.

"Arn?" Slurne hiccupped, his voice as small as a child's.

For a flicker of a moment, Pickett had the horrible image of the man leaping to his feet and running to his friend. That image was followed by the gruesome scene in her mind. She made to hold Slurne back, but before she could even reach him, his confused, owlish blink transformed into an expression of unrestrained horror. The blood drained from his face, leaving it bone pale just before a sickly green seeped into his cheeks. He rolled over and spewed out the rum and whatever else he'd eaten that day in great, lumpy yellow globs before he staggered to his feet. Even drunk, he had the good sense to know what was a friend and what was a nightmare from the pits of horror.

The Arn-thing swayed for a moment, then took a step forward. Slurne yelped and jumped back, one of his heels sliding in the pile of sick, which sent him slamming back down onto the floor. Pickett started back, reaching automatically for Edie. Not that Edie needed her protection. Not by a longshot. After a frightened screech, Edie snatched one of the wooden mugs from the counter and hurled it.

That was apparently all the Arn thing needed. It let out a wet roar, pinkish froth foaming on its lips as it lumbered forward, its mismatched eyes latched onto its former friend.

Any confusion or shock that kept the other patrons in place dissolved. Screams filled the space as traders and fishermen scrambled for the back door. One screeched particularly loudly as a rotted board split under his foot, pitching one leg straight down into the murky swamp waters. He struggled to pull himself back out, but he couldn't quite manage it around the many other feet pounding around him, all abandoning the Pick's Pocket to its grisly fate.

As they fled, one patron turned and hoisted a stool like a weapon with one hand and a raised a half-eaten potato shim with the other.

"No!" Pickett yelled, but all she could do was watch with a sinking heart as the delicious treasure sailed through the air, splatting against the Arn-thing's face. His bulging eye popped out with a squelch and dangled like a fishing lure. It snarled louder, blood dribbling like jelly from its lips, changing direction.

"What have you summoned, witch?" the enforcer shouted, and the Arn-thing's head whipped back around.

This was starting to give Pickett an inkling of an idea. Before she could act on it, the enforcer's strong hand closed around her arm, shoving her forward toward the thing. Pickett bucked and kicked back against him, but clearly this guy knew how to hold someone against their will. He pushed her between the Arn-thing and himself, shifting whenever she tried to buck back against him.

The Arn-thing shot forward, wrapping its hands around her neck. Pickett kicked out against his leg, which squelched putrid water under her heel. The skin of his leg ripped and peeled, but his bones remained as strong as ever.

She coughed and gasped as the grip tightened and tightened, accompanied by snarls. Fuck the fish, the Arn-thing was absolutely murderous! Was this truly how she was going to die? No, it couldn't be. It wouldn't be. She croaked, jerking violently against him as dark spots danced before her eyes.

Just as the dark threatened to overtake the light, something hot sprayed against the back of her neck, followed by a gurgle and a groan. The enforcer's heavy weight sagged, dropping her to the floor and popping her free from the Arn-thing's grasp— along with one of its waterlogged thumbs.

It bellowed, just as something blurred through the air, knocking into it with a swishing burst of water and blood and other meaty bits. Bodies swirled above her with broken chair bits and planks, murmuring to each other as they worked above her at . . . What were they doing? Oh fuck. They were completely dismembering the undead Arn. In her bar. That couldn't be sanitary. Not that the Pick's Pocket had ever been the picture of cleanliness, but this crossed a line.

Pickett blinked, the black spots growing smaller as her sight returned, revealing Edie among the figures above her. Dark splotches of red sprayed the front of her lovely bodice. Oh no, they didn't even have enough money for new shoes. How would they replace Edie's bodice? And her skirt! It was stained too.

Pickett blinked sadly before her senses began to come back to her. That was blood on Edie's front, which meant that was blood on Pickett's back and blood seeping from the enforcer she was laying on and . . .

She rolled over, pushing herself up on one elbow, eyes wide. "Fuck!"

The enforcer shuddered on the ground, the red blood pooling like a massive red cloak behind him, his mouth bobbing for a few moments before his eyes went glossy and still like painted marbles. A knife stuck right out of his neck. A knife with a rough, splintery handle–the best Pickett could afford for this dump.

She stared up at Edie with wide eyes. Edie stared back at her. No, they'd sworn it wouldn't happen again. Pickett had promised Edie that after the last time, it would never happen again. It was Pickett's hands that would be dirty. Edie was never supposed to have to lift a finger in violence or anger for the rest of her life.

What had she done?

"Edie," Pickett wheezed around the jagged rocks in her throat as she clambered to her feet.

Edie stared down at the body of the enforcer without shock or terror or rage. Just resignation. Like she'd been trying to hold back floodwaters and they broke through anyway. Edie had killed him. For Pickett. No, because of Pickett. Because of Pickett, he was here in the first place.

She reached for her, but Edie backed away, arms wrapped around her waist.

"We should secure the door," she said.

Right. She was right. Most of the bar was empty, but they were still here, along with Slurne and the youngish fisherman whose leg had gone through the floor but was now free. That was four of them who still needed to get through the night.

Pickett nodded. "Yeah. We should."

"Hold on." Slurne's voice sounded rough. He grabbed the enforcer by his ankles and began yanking him. His wet shoe squelching as he moved, the young fisherman grabbed the dead enforcer's arms and helped Slurne. Maybe it was the air loss, or maybe Pickett was an even bigger dunderhead than she realized, because she didn't quite realize what they were doing until they reached the door.

"Wait, don't."

But the sound of a heavy splash cut her off.

"NO!" Pickett lurched forward, shoving the patrons out of the way as she stumbled onto the boardwalk. But it was too late. The enforcer was in the water. How long until he too rose up with an even nastier attitude and an penchant for violence? What else would join him when he inevitably did come for them?

The waters roiled with life. No. Not life. They roiled with whatever un-life had been building up in them this whole time.

"Those fish'll make short work of that bastard's body," Slurne growled. "And-and Arn too." His voice hitched a little, but Pickett had already used up all her pity on the only person who mattered. And that wasn't Slurne.

"Get back inside," she growled. "Get something to bar the door."

To their credit, Slurne and the other fellow didn't argue, and they left Pickett alone in the door of the Pick's Pocket to gaze out at the chaos boiling under the surface. The dead were rising, they were angry, and they were going to be a lot more dangerous than a single asshole fish.

No charm, no con could fix this. This was fucking magic and she had nothing up her sleeve to deal with it. They could try making a run for the village. Abandon the bar and go somewhere safe. But as Pickett gazed at the nearest land, the tree line seemed to shrink away, impossibly far with the fury of the dead along the path. She had no idea how many of her patrons had made it to safety, but she'd bet her last coin that more than one had fallen. Fleeing would be an ugly risk.

In the distance, a figure walked along the docks, slow and steady. Either he didn't know the danger or he didn't care. Well. He'd die or make it to her. Pickett narrowed her eyes, then sucked in a sharp breath when she realized it was the bounty hunter, and he had Letterboy in tow.

CHAPTER

THIRTEEN

All the despair and exhaustion inside of her crystallized into a single, pointed rage. That bastard had the stupid kid, and he dared to let her see it. At a time when she really, really could not handle one more thing in her life going to shit.

Edie might never speak to her again. Her home would soon be overrun by the dead and she could think of no good way out. There was no solution to those in front of her. But the hunter had just given her something she could take her rage and anger out on.

With a snarl, Pickett stomped back inside, right to the kitchen in the back. Edie sat on a stool, shoulders hunched over, utterly miserable. Utterly miserable because Pickett was a feckless idiot.

Edie's head shot up. Her eyes were red. Her cheeks were splotched. The expression on her face was a morph of fear and anger.

Pickett snatched a knife from the block and set her jaw.

"I fucked up," she announced. Well, croaked through a damaged throat. As if Edie needed to have the obvious confirmed. "I fucked up and I don't know if I can make it right. But I promised nobody would come for you, and I meant it."

Edie's mouth opened, but this wasn't the time for a heart-to-heart. Or verbal lashing to ear, rather. Pickett turned on her heel, stalking back to the door, where Slurne and the young fisherman were in the process of shoving tables and chairs up against it.

"Move these," she ordered.

"But you said—"

"Now!"

The men shared a nervous glance, then went about un-blocking the entrance, at least enough for Pickett to pass. The second she stepped out onto the boardwalk, however, the water below churned and frothed violently. A flash of scales and teeth shot up before sinking back down.

Pickett backed up and gritted her teeth. Well, if she ran fast enough, they couldn't get her. At least not until after she took this particular bastard down. She'd be damned if he was going to put Letterboy or Edie through anything more.

She charged out onto the rickety boardwalk. Whatever gods may have deigned to sneeze in her direction at some point in her life surely must have ensured that her attempts to patch the worst of the rot would hold because nothing snapped or gave beyond an ominous creak. It just had to hold out long enough for her to slit this bastard's throat before he could take Edie in, before he could do whatever he was planning to do with Letterboy.

Something below the water surged up, taking out half the boardwalk with its scaly head. A swamp beast. She'd never seen one in person but of course she knew they existed. They'd always been around, swimming beneath the surface. Its gray, mottled snout jutted out from an angular face, sharp teeth sticking out of the gaps in its ruined jaw. Even its back was scaled with spikes. Every inch of it had been built to kill. And yet something somewhere had killed it first.

All right. New plan. Kill this thing first. Then kill the bounty hunter. Then try not to die.

She stared into its cloudy eyes for a long minute. It stared back, so motionless a part of her hoped the magic had seeped out of it and it sagged back down into the waters. Until, with a hiss, it shot forward.

Pickett skipped out of the way and brought the knife down hard, slashing out one of its eyes. The beast snarked and yanked back, clotted blood dribbling from the wound for a second before it rammed back into her. Pickett staggered, almost toppling off the edge of the boardwalk before she caught her footing.

With a whistle, a bolt shot through the air, piercing straight through the beast's other eye and into the place where its brain ought to be. It hissed and thrashed, jutting back into the water. Some part of it must have slammed into one of the supports. The shake of wood beneath her feet toppled her already tenuous balance, and Pickett slipped through the air toward the water.

Huh. So this was how she died. Slipping and falling right on top of a swamp beast. Maybe it'd make a good story. Maybe even a song. Pity she wouldn't get to hear it.

Before she felt the splash of water around her and the jaws of death, a hand yanked at the front of her shirt. Pickett came to an abrupt halt, her neck snapping backward then forward. She stared up into the eyes of the bounty hunter, crossbow held aloft in one of his hands.

Without the faintest wisp of a thought, Pickett's arm shot up, pressing the gunky-blood-covered blade against his exposed throat.

His eyes widened, but he didn't release her shirt. Nor did he fully haul her back up onto the busted boardwalk.

"Quite the thank you for someone who just saved your life."

Pickett scowled. Without taking her eyes off him, she called out, "Letterboy? Are you all right?"

Out of the corner of her eye, she saw his small, disheveled figure poke out from behind the bounty hunter. "I was coming to warn you. Someone was coming. But something jumped out of the water and he saved me."

Pickett sighed. She had to hand it to him. The kid was brave. "Yeah. Fistic's enforcer. But you didn't have to risk it, Letterboy. Edie and I took care of him."

And apparently this bounty hunter had saved Letterboy. Pickett looked him up and down, but she couldn't quite relax around him.

Letterboy shuddered. "C-can we get to the Pick's Pocket? Please?"

The bounty hunter jerked his head toward Letterboy. "You gonna keep the kid out here with the swamp beasts?"

Pickett's lip curled. "Letterboy, hurry on ahead. Find Edie. She'll feed you."

He didn't need to be told twice. Quick as a bolt, Letterboy took off down the boardwalk. Even the wind couldn't have hoped to catch him.

The bounty hunter scowled down at her. "You clearly have trust issues."

"You clearly came into my bar asking questions you shouldn't have been asking."

He arched a brow. "Is that so?"

Pickett put a little more pressure on the knife.

The bounty hunter huffed. "You slice my throat, I drop you in the swamp. How long until that beast comes back for another shot?"

"At least the people in my bar will be safe from you."

The water churned under her. Something smacked against Pickett's back. Was it her fish, or just one of the many myriads of dead creatures who lived in the swamp?

She stared up at him and waited. She didn't slice his throat. He didn't drop her in the water. Clearly, he wanted her alive more than he wanted an unscarred throat. She just needed to lean on this.

"Give me your crossbow," she demanded.

"My what?"

Pickett grabbed the front of his shirt, just to give herself a little extra security. And because her stomach was starting to ache from her position.

"Give me your crossbow and you can walk into the Pick's Pocket. You can even keep the bolts."

"Why, so you can knock me out when I'm not looking?"

"It's that or we both stay here until that beast comes back."

With a low growl, the bounty hunter hauled Pickett back up onto the boardwalk. She stumbled, losing her close hold on his throat. She whirled around, prepared for him to take advantage of the slip-up and jump her, wrestle her knife away, maybe even do to her what she'd tried to do to him. But instead, he pulled a bolt out of his crossbow, tucking it into a little quiver on his thigh before handing it over.

"Nobody warned me you could be such a bitch."

Pickett smirked, snatching it out of his hand. "Witch. Bitch. I'm the one with the crossbow."

CHAPTER

FOURTEEN

When they reached the bar, a table had already been turned on its side and pressed against the gaping hole that had once been a door.

Pickett ground her teeth and shouted, "Move that thing or I'll turn you idiots to toads!"

The bounty hunter's head turned just a little, but he said nothing. The table rolled out of the way and Pickett prodded his back with the crossbow, ushering him inside. Slurne and the other patron rolled the table back before they braced a few chairs clumsily behind it. Well, carpenters and builders weren't exactly her usual clientele.

"You," she snapped, gesturing toward the young fisherman with the patchy beard.

"Deggir."

"Deggir." Pickett jerked her head toward the kitchen. "Do you know how to tie a knot?"

"For hitching a mule, sure."

"Good enough. You'll tie our friend here to one of the support beams. After you push one of the tables over your hole from earlier."

"Wasn't my hole. It was the fucking monster's hole," Deggir muttered, but he shuffled off to do as he was told.

The bounty hunter rolled his eyes but wisely kept his trap shut. Pickett narrowed her eyes. He seemed far too calm about this, but she didn't have time to play mind games with him.

"Slurne, go with him to get some rope," Pickett barked. "There should be some in the kitchen."

Slurne's mouth opened, but he must have thought better of what he was going to say because he shut it and hurried to follow her orders. The thought of two people who were not Edie rummaging around in the kitchen made Pickett's stomach turn like she'd just gulped a cup of swamp crab stew, but it was better than leaving one of them to keep an eye on the bounty hunter. The steady thump of something smacking up against the floorboards chased away any fears about privacy. For now, they needed to make it through the night. And then maybe the next day. And then . . . fuck. Pickett would focus on the night and then each minute after as it came.

Edie examined Letterboy's injured finger. "Oh, your hands are filthy. We may need to rip up clean rags for bandages. No sense in you coming all this way and losing that finger."

Pickett spared a quick glance over Edie's shoulder to get a better look. Had the kid gone and picked at the scab to reopen it? Children were disgusting. Wait. Wait, shit, what had Hoag said?

"Find some clean rags too!" she shouted to the men in the kitchen.

"No rags in here!" Deggir shouted.

"In the drawer by the stove."

There came a loud crash which may or may not have been the cabinet of their pewter and wood dishes, then the two men returned triumphantly from the kitchen; Deggir brandished a coil of rope, Slurne an old rag. With a sigh, the bounty hunter backed up, allowing Deggir to tie him to one of the support columns.

"This is really not necessary," he said dryly. "I've obviously proven I don't mean you any harm. Not that I could do anything to harm such a powerful"—his lip twitched—"witch."

The word sent a chill down Pickett's spine.

"Make it tight," she ordered before kneeling next to Edie and Letterboy, who had his hand out. And her stomach might have smacked the floor at the sight of his fish-bitten finger. No. He hadn't lost it, but Hoag's words suddenly made more sense.

"What in the name of cheap booze?" Pickett muttered.

Letterboy's finger was red and puffy, with blood dribbling out from a few puncture wounds. But it wasn't the red and puffy of a wound several days old. It looked like he'd been freshly bitten.

Thumps sounded against the floorboards right underneath them. A reminder of exactly what had given Letterboy that particular wound.

"It isn't healing," Edie said grimly. "It hasn't even started healing."

"I promise I kept it bandaged up." Letterboy sniffed. "But it just kept hurting and I thought wh-what if all my blood just poured out and I-I went to the apothecary to see if he could help me. But he couldn't. So I thought—"

"You thought I could heal you." Pickett glanced up at Edie, who set her jaw and glared back. Of course she was furious. She had every right. But in that moment, they had bigger undead fish to fry.

"Well?" the bounty hunter called. "Is the witch of the swamp going to do something? Heal the child? Save us all from the undead?"

A chill filled the air. Pickett pulled out the knife and rose. The bounty hunter had been bound, but he slouched back against the column, completely calm. He might as well have asked to be tied up.

Slurne shifted from one foot to the other.

"You have something to say?" Pickett snapped.

"Well, aren't you?" Slurne gestured at the badly barricaded door. "You said you brought that fish from the beyond. Maybe it, I dunno, infected everything."

"Or maybe I'm not the only sorcerer around. Did you think of that?" She turned, pointed the dagger at the bounty hunter. "This fellow's new around here. Maybe he's riding my coat tails. Making chaos from an honest bit of magic."

It wasn't a great defense but, sometimes, reasonable doubt was just enough to keep someone alive. Pickett rubbed the back of her neck.

"It's not supposed to affect anyone living on the land but fuck. Looks like we're fucked if we're injured by these things. So this other sorcerer, who definitely exists, might want to cause chaos."

"Quite the accusation." The bounty hunter arched a brow. "You know nothing about me."

"Slurne, Deggir, go double check on our stocks in the larder. I think we have some bandages stuffed in there," Pickett ordered as she stalked forward and rested the knife right back where it belonged, dancing on the apple of the county hunter's throat.

"I know you're here to threaten one of mine," she warned. "I don't take well to that."

"And yet you haven't killed me."

Thump. Thump. Thump.

The undead smacking against the floorboards set Pickett's teeth on edge. She gripped the knife a little tighter.

"You saved me from the swamp beast. One good turn deserves a hesitation before I stab you."

"Quite the temper." The bounty hunter shifted, leaning forward until Pickett was forced to pull back the knife just a hair before she did cut his throat. And the hunter knew it. He narrowed his eyes. "Tell me. Are you a murderer yourself or just in the habit of harboring them?"

Fuck. How did he know that? Pickett adjusted her grip on the knife and stared right into his icy eyes. She could do it. If she had to, she'd do it. Even if she had to slit his throat right there in front of everyone.

"What bounty on a milkmaid could possibly be worth coming out here in the middle of an attack of the dead?"

"Huh?" the bounty hunter blinked.

"Pickett please!" Edie cried out. "I think maybe this conversation would go better if you didn't have a knife to his throat."

"Yes, Pickett," the bounty hunter echoed. "I think I'm less your enemy than the things swimming in the water around us."

"Who sent you after her?" Pickett snarled, pressing the knife forward.

This time, the bounty hunter moved, pressing back against the column. His eyes flicked over Pickett's shoulder, then back.

"The girl? I don't even know who she is."

"Wait. What?"

For a long, confusing moment, they stared at each other, and Pickett genuinely wasn't sure if she ought to be confused or threatened in that moment. By the look of him, the bounty hunter didn't know, either.

"So we've got three tater shims, a box of the tack, and some sort of dried berries," Slurne cut in as he returned from the kitchen. "Oh. You two still trying to kill each other?"

"Unclear," Pickett muttered.

The bounty hunter pursed his lips. "So did you kill Marnoc or is he just not here?"

Wait. "Marnoc?"

"Marnoc of Gallraven." The bounty hunter furrowed his brows. "He disappeared right after he murdered his brother. Chased some girl out here. Folk think he killed her too."

All this time, he hadn't been after Edie at all. He'd been after a dead man.

"Oh shit," Pickett breathed.

"Oh shit," Edie hissed before, with a thump and a crash, something broke through the wood. Pickett whirled around, holding the knife out.

"Ow, fuck, you nicked me!" the bounty hunter shouted, but he shut up the second they all saw the skeletal hand, bits of bloated skin still clinging to the knuckles, clawing through the floorboards and right toward Edie.

FIFTEEN

If Pickett had to list out every indescribably fucked moment of her life, she would never have predicted a bloated, skeletal arm reaching for her kitchen maid would take the top. A week or so ago, she wouldn't have even considered it would be part of the list. A week ago, Pickett would have thought the most indescribably fucked parts of her life were behind her. But she was now a week older, a week wiser, and a lifetime more fucked. And it was getting worse by the second. A second arm shot out of the water, this one a little more fleshy, with a few tiny fish still gnawing at the decaying flesh until they fell back into the water.

And it was going after Edie.

Pickett threw herself to the ground, stabbing at one of those hands again and again with the knife. Squelches of mud and old blood gushed out of the hand. But as the half-decayed head rose from the water, its empty eye sockets turned to her.

Pickett was really hitting fresh peaks of fuckitude.

She scrambled back, but the skeletal hand lashed out, grabbing at her ankle with a strength that didn't exactly fit with something so decayed. Pickett screeched and kicked out her leg, trying to shake it off. But the thing that had once been Marnoc let out a guttural growl, slapping his other arm onto her leg as he either tried to pull himself up or her down into the abyss of the swamp with him.

Shouts came from the men, but Pickett couldn't hear them over the growing ringing in her ears as that horrible maw gnashed what teeth remained at her. Pickett twisted onto her side, kicking with her other leg as hard as she could. There was an awful snap as Marnoc's head jerked back, right before he closed his jaw around the toe of her boot.

"Son of a bitch."

Pickett tried rolling to break the monster's grasp on her, but he just sloshed in the water, holding tight and biting all the harder until she could feel the pressure of those teeth on her toe.

"You useless sacks of shit, do something!" Pickett shouted, sliding the knife across the floor at Slurne and Deggir.

Slurne picked it up, his hand trembling so violently she feared he might stab himself. Then he proceeded to not charge forward and try to help her extricate herself. The bounty hunter shouted something at him, but he just glanced helplessly from him to Pickett, then back down to the blade, as though repeating the same motion again and again might shake loose whatever was blocking his brain from functioning.

Worse, as Pickett twisted and rolled over, she saw Edie. The blood drained from her face. At some point, something had ripped her pink skirt up to her knee. She didn't move. Her eyes fixed on the undead head, staring and snarling at Pickett as it gnawed on her shoe. Did she see the man who tormented her? Did she see her own guilt? Her death?

For one wonderful, horrible, drunken moment, Pickett was back in that night, dead drunk because there were no customers so there was no reason not to be. Then a radiant beam of a creature burst in, followed by an oaf of a man. Pickett was pretty sure she'd helped, but all she'd been able to do, in the end, was watch in awe as that beautiful young woman had bludgeoned her attacker into unconsciousness. She'd helped Pickett tie him up, drag him out, and ultimately made the decision to shove his still-breathing body into the murky depths of the Rottering swamp. She was everything Pickett had wanted to be. She was everything Pickett wanted around her.

But here she was, regressed to a frightened creature cowering, staring at the thing holding on to Pickett as if it was Edie, not Pickett, having her foot chewed upon. And son of a bitch, if that didn't piss her off all the more. Edie should have been fierce. She should have been angry!

"Edie, get the fuck out of here!" Pickett shouted, but Edie didn't respond. Pickett growled inwardly and rolled again. There was a pop and a gush of thick, muddy blood as something came loose. Pickett pulled one foot free to see the skeletal hand still clinging to it, free of the arm. The Marnoc-thing continued to chew on her boot, but with only one hand with which to cling, it was beginning to slip back into the water.

Pickett rolled again, this time swiftly enough to break the grip of the good hand. The Marnoc-thing released a wet, guttural roar and clawed at the wood as Pickett scrambled back, yanking the amputated hand from her leg. It tried to twist and grasp at her, but she hurled it across the room before it could twist around and grasp at her wrist.

As it turned out, this was exactly the right course of action and, as much as Pickett thought she might be an idiot, perhaps she ought to reconsider that she was secretly a genius. Because the hand smacked Edie right in the face. Edie jerked, blood and mud smearing across her cheek as she screeched and hurled the hand across the bar before scrambling back, finally free of her fear-born paralysis.

Pickett clambered to her feet and staggered back. Only then

could she finally make out what the bounty hunter had been shouting the whole time.

"Bolts! Bolts for the love of Slaggo's crooked teeth. Bolts!"

Oh. Oh! She hurried to the captive bounty hunter, who had switched from commands to a veritable slurry of swears. In fact, it would have been absolutely impressive had Pickett not been in such a hurry. She snatched up a handful of bolts and the fallen crossbow.

Despite being one handed down, the Marnoc-thing had clambered up into the bar, half his torso on the floor as he continued to snarl and sneer.

Her hands shook as she tried to thread the bolt into the bow. She sucked in a sharp breath and tried to pretend the bolts were her powders. That too much sudden movements would send them off.

Slurn and Deggir were still as helpful as sugar-coated shits. From across the room, Edie's eyes switched from terror to a softened sort of rage.

Pickett tried and failed to properly thread the bolt.

Edie grabbed a chair from one of the tables. At last, her anger was taking hold.

Pickett tried and failed again to thread the bolt as Edie screeched, "Bastard!" and swung the chair at the Marnoc-thing.

Splinters. Broken chunks of wood. A loud crack. It was all very heroic, but apparently they indeed felt no pain. The monster didn't even seem to notice the fresh gash in its head, complete with a massive chunk of wood sticking out from its temple as it lunged forward, its good hand grasping her ankle.

"Edie!"

Pickett dropped a bolt and scrambled for another. The creature jerked at Edie's foot, dragging her to the ground. Edie screamed, but that fight was back. She grasped a broken leg chair and desperately tried to stab him anywhere she could.

At last, the bold clicked into place. Pickett held the crossbow up.

Fwip!

Thunk!

Fuck! It lodged itself into the wood just over the creature's head. She tried again. It only graced the creature's back as it pulled itself up, finally grasping at Edie's bodice. Then her throat.

No.

No!

Pickett threaded another bolt and, this time, it clicked into place immediately. She leveled it at the creature's head and fired. Then she fired again. And a third time. One by one, the bolts shot through his skull, spraying mostly-congealed blood and mud onto the floor behind him until, at last, he released his grip.

Edie jumped to her feet and shoved the moving corpse toward the hole he cam eout of. Then she ran away as she should have forever ago. Pickett threaded another bolt. The next to last. Already, the Marnoc-thing had three in its skull. Drool and jelly-like blood dribbled from its lips, but it continued crawling in the direction that Edie had fled.

Pickett raised the crossbow, focusing harder this time.

Fwip!

Thunk!

The next-to-last bolt pinned the creature in place, half in and half out of the water. All right. It was gruesome, but she could work with this. Pickett held out one hand and was about to call for a knife when Edie returned, grasping the massive cleaver they only used with hefty hunks of meat. The sort they were seldom generous enough to sell to customers.

Pickett could only jump back as Edie fell to her knees and screeched, bringing the cleaver down again and again, first to the monster's neck. Then his shoulder. Then his wrist. Most of him sank back into the swamp. It kicked and jerked, but could do no more than splash fetid water onto the half-rotted wood. The hand strained under the knife. The arm twitched on the floor. The mouth gnashed its teeth. But it couldn't hurt anyone.

Well. Sort of.

Edie's hand shook. Her eyes filled with tears as the cleaver shook in her hand. She glanced at Pickett, then swiftly away, letting it fall to the floor as she retreated a few steps.

Right. Well, that was something to deal with later. Edie would be fine. She was always fine.

Pickett ducked behind the bar, snatching up the cleaning bucket. It still had a lump of tallow-soap at the bottom, but if Marnoc hated the scent, then all the better. She carried it over, grabbing the gnashing head by its hairs. A few snapped upon her first grasp, but just enough of them held for her to drop it into the bucket, followed by the arm, followed by the hand with the knife in it.

Pickett heaved a deep breath, planting her hands on her hips as she stared down at it. It would be pretty hard for those few bits of him to crawl out and continue making trouble.

"All right," she announced, sliding the bucket toward the still-bound bounty hunter. "There's your target."

The bounty hunter dropped his chin. It was hard to tell if he was about to cry or vomit. All too often, the two went hand in hand.

"I won't get two shims for this nonsense," he muttered.

Well, good to know he had his priorities in place. Pickett could respect that. She shrugged.

"Pity to be a pauper."

SIXTEEN

While Marnoc's dismembered lower half kicked ineffectually under the water, more swamp creatures tried to clamber into the bar. The front half of a snapping turtle, a water snake with part of its spine showing, and even a cat. How a cat managed to get this deep into the swamp, Pickett didn't know, but she swung the crossbow like a club, knocking it back into the water with a feral yowl along with the other beasts. All the while, her ankle stung.

"Come on," Edie said, ripping up some of the cleaner rags and retrieving a bottle of rum from behind the bar.

"Fine." Pickett gestured at Deggir. "You. Turn over one of the tables and cover up this hole. Slurne, go ahead and cut that asshole loose. We gave him what he came for."

They probably didn't particularly enjoy being bossed around like that, but Pickett didn't really enjoy having undead creatures climbing up through the hole in her floor. So it was a little mollifying to know that everyone was unhappy. Deggir cut the bounty hunter free. Said bounty hunter staggered forward, shooting a filthy look at the bucket with Marnoc's head before giving Pickett a filthy gesture. Pickett returned it as she settled on one of the barstools and held her ankle out.

Edie didn't make eye contact as she splashed some of the rum onto Pickett's wound. The fiery sting on her ankle was almost refreshing. It gave her something else to focus on.

Surely, though, there had to be something she could do or say or, fuck, become if it meant she could win back some of Edie's trust. But what were her options, exactly? She could explain why she'd kept truth about Fistic to herself. She could promise never to keep another secret like that again. If Pickett truly wanted to be daring, she could even try to become an honest person. The thought made her skin crawl just a little, but she'd do it if it could just make Edie look at her!

Instead, Edie stared hard at Pickett's ankle as she wrapped the ribbons of rag around it, firm and even. What was going through her head? It was torment staring at her and not knowing. Was she angry? Disappointed? Plotting how best to slit Pickett's throat when she wasn't looking?

With a sigh, Pickett forced herself to glance at something else. Letterboy stood nearby, picking at his wounded finger.

"Hey," she barked, gesturing for him. "Quit picking at that."

"It's not like I'll stop it from healing."

"No but you'll make it worse. Let me see it."

Stiffly, Letterboy shuffled toward her, but he didn't exactly hand over his finger. So Pickett had to grab his wrist and drag him closer. Sure enough, the skin around the wound was inflamed and bleeding in more spots, now, than just the fish bite. He must have been picking at it all this time. And it was filthy.

"What is this?" she scoffed, plucking at something that looked like a stray hair or sliver of grass.

Letterboy yelped, jumping back as whatever it was resisted Pickett's tug, then finally came free with a couple of drops of blood. Pickett wrinkled her nose.

"Was this inside your finger?"

Letterboy looked like he was about to vomit. Pickett frowned and held the little curl of whatever it was up as Edie finished, dropping her ankle like a sack of flour.

"It looks like moss," she mused. "How did moss get that deep in your finger?"

"Shouldn't you know, madame sorcerer?" The bounty hunter sidled up to the bar, tugging the rum bottle from Edie's hands and sniffing before taking a slug for himself. "That's the stuff. Don't know why you'd mix this with your foul juice."

"I need that." Edie tugged the bottle back with just a little extra force before heading over to Letterboy. "Come on. Let's at least get it cleaned and bandaged."

With that, she caught Letterboy's elbow, leading him to the corner in the back of the bar, pausing only to shoot Pickett and the bounty hunter a glare. It made Pickett's insides shrivel like seaweed left out in the sun. The bounty hunter glanced from Edie, then back to Pickett.

"Did you two kill Marnoc, or did he happen to die and rot under the establishment of two people who happened to know him?"

Pickett leaned over the bar to grab a fresh bottle of rum. It was only half full. Pity. If she was going to lose her livelihood and possibly die ripped to shreds by the undead, she'd have very much preferred to do so while blind drunk. She poured it into one of the glasses abandoned by the earlier patrons and took a long pull. She waited until the fire died down in her nose and the back of her throat before she trusted herself to answer.

"Personally, I'd say breathing in swamp water killed him. But we certainly didn't do him any favors."

"Mm. Interesting." The bounty hunter reached for the bottle, but Pickett slid just out of his reach. He scowled and drummed his fingers on the bar top. "I find it very interesting that a woman of your supposed considerable power didn't burn the body to ash right there."

"I had a busy night." Pickett took another long pull of rum. It took a moment, but it was finally starting to pleasantly numb her brain.

"She didn't use her magic earlier, either," Slurne cut in.

Pickett shot him a look as filthy as the water around them, enough to force Slurne to take a step back. But Deggir strode up next to him, brows so furrowed they might have been stitched together.

"But I saw it," he said. "She summoned fire on the stage."

"But not against the creatures," Slurne said.

"Interesting," the bounty hunter drawled, a wide grin stretching across his face.

"The fuck do you want?" Pickett hissed.

"You're right." Deggir breathed. "Maybe she used all her power up. Or maybe it couldn't work on them."

"What a question," the hunter said, rising from his seat. "It does make one wonder what she's keeping from us. What else she might be hiding."

"She's the one who brought all the dead things back!" Slurne spouted, jumping forward.

Ice ran through Pickett's veins. Oh fuck.

The bounty hunter turned toward her. "Makes me wonder what else this sorceress is hiding. And what else she knows."

"This isn't my fault!" She glanced around quickly.

Pickett held up the bottle, dancing between options. She could take another long drink and numb all this horrible shit, but abandon her wits. Or she could keep sharp and painful.

Slurne pointed at her with a shaking finger. "She had a dead fish. She charged money for us to see it. She told us she brought it back from the other side."

"And why would you bring back the dead when you knew the

bastard you killed was rotting under your bar?" the bounty hunter demanded.

Pickett stared at his sharp eyes, already seeing too much and looking for more. She looked at Slurne, who didn't seem to see his bartender. He saw a monster. She looked at Deggir who, well, frankly, she knew jack all about him and didn't really give a shit what he thought.

And Edie and Letterboy were on the other side of the bar, deep in conversation. Because Edie was pissed. Because Pickett lied. Because Pickett was a liar and a shitty person who just created these situations herself.

She knocked back the remainder of the rum and slammed the glass back down on the bar.

"I didn't bring them back," she snapped.

The bar fell silent, save for the periodic thump of angry dead things against the floor of Pick's Pocket.

"You're lying," Slurne whispered.

The bounty hunter straightened, his grin so self-satisfied he would have easily fit in with the dead cat bobbing around in the swamp beneath them. "For once, I think we have the truth."

Was all of this vengeance because he found out Marnoc was dead? Was he angry she threatened him? Or was he just trying to goad her into revealing something he could use to make money? For his sake, she hoped he didn't think he could win a bounty off of her. Who in any known or unknown world would drop a single pip on a bounty for the likes of her? Fistic, for his part, would just wait for her to die and send someone else to ransack the bar for anything of value she might have.

Pickett took a deep breath, waiting for the rum to fog her brain just a little more.

"I didn't bring the fish back. I took advantage of it when I found it." She paused, glancing back at Slurne. "I wouldn't use my power for something like that."

"Gods above." The bounty hunter groaned, while Deggir and Slurne hissed and whispered amongst themselves.

Maybe it was just the rum in her brain, but Pickett couldn't help noticing that she sat in the middle of a very interesting situation. All three men around her thought she was lying. But they did not appear to agree on what, exactly, her lie even was.

Slurne and Deggir looked like frightened mice, trying to decide where to scurry to protect themselves.

The bounty hunter looked like a mother with an exhausting toddler.

Best to try to straddle the one undeniable truth between them.

"Look. We have a problem in the swamp that I can't solve. But if we can just make it through the night—"

"Liar." Deggir growled.

Pickett glared at him. "Yes. Thank you. I think we can all agree I'm a liar."

"So if you can't stop them," he said. "Then maybe the person who brought them back needs to die to send them back to the afterlife."

Pickett growled, reaching for the bottle of rum. "I told you, I—"

Her fingers only just brushed against the glass before it disappeared. She blinked, only a moment before something heavy smashed into the side of her head. Pain burst out like an explosion. Stars flooded her vision. Pickett cried out a second before she felt arms around her middle, dragging her off the stool.

Shouts broke through the air from Edie, Letterboy, and even the bounty hunter.

Rum and pain swirled together, smothering rational thought. Wood scraped against wood as cool water slapped her back, followed by the sound of splashing. The last thing Pickett heard was Edie screaming her name before the swamp enveloped her.

Don't breathe!

Pickett's head throbbed. Her body drifted. But her mind still functioned well enough to screech that she could not breathe, no matter how much her chest burned.

She reached out her arm and kicked, praying that she was facing upward. Just as her fingers brushed against slimy wood, something wrapped around her waist. Pickett screamed, precious air bubbling out of her mouth and floating away as whatever it was tried to drag her down. Or maybe it was trying to use her to climb up.

Pickett wriggled against the thing that had her waist, but it only tightened its grip. But it didn't hurt. Not yet.

She blinked, straining to see through the thick mass of her own dark hair floating in the murky, grainy water around her and twisted around to get a better look at her attacker. Strange. Part of her had sort of assumed it was the enforcer coming back remarkably swiftly. Through the thin streaks of light that cut through from the slats in the floorboards, she could see bones, held together by wiry sinews. The light illuminated a skull, a rip, a hip. And it just floated there, its empty eye sockets angled up toward her. And that was all it did. It just held her and floated. What, were they suddenly not murderous when they were in the swamp water? That paled next to the more serious question: just how many bodies had been dumped out here over the years?

With her urgency fading away, Pickett slammed her foot squarely into its bony face. Its jaw fell open as it let go just enough to grasp her cape hem. Pickett probably could have fought it, but her chest was growing tight. So, with a pang of regret, she shrugged out of her precious, colorful cape and watched as it and the old bones drifted off, claimed by the darkness of the swamp.

The sudden weightlessness sent Pickett floating back up to the base of the bar. She reached up, groping at the slimy wood until she felt splinters. She could have heaved a sigh of relief if she had enough breath leftover to spare. She kicked up, but her hands only met wood. Less slimy. More sticky. The wood of a table.

Those cocksuckers!

She hoped Edie was giving them what for. And, at the same time, she hoped she wasn't. Not if they were frightened enough to hurl people out into the swamp.

Her chest tightened, a burn of fire flooding her lungs. Her head throbbed. But she needed to think. If this was where the hole was, then she just needed to swim until she could find somewhere she could breathe.

Pickett bit the inside of her cheek and began pushing through, ignoring the faint, grit of mud and sand in her eyes as she moved too slowly toward where the boardwalks had to be.

Something else moved in the water. Only in the feeble light filtering down from the outside of the bar could she pinpoint the details. It was long, like a lizard or a serpent with a horrible snout. Her mind was all too horribly happy to fill in all the other details: scales and rows of knife-like teeth.

Pickett had to slam her hand over her mouth to stop from screaming. The swamp beast was back. Of course it was. The bounty hunter had only scared it off. She couldn't possibly fight it off in its own territory. Oh gods, when it killed her, how long would it take until she too came back as some angry, undead creature? Would she attack Edie? Letterboy?

She only just managed to swallow her panic enough to push lower in the water. Her lungs screamed in protest, but there was nothing else she could do for it. She had to at least try not to die, if only for them. As she tried to reason out the best place to attack if it came toward her.

Instead, it swam overhead, giving her a full view of its pale, rotting belly. A small school of living fish followed it, periodically flapping upward to nibble at the bits of decaying flesh that hung off of it like fraying linen. Did it not notice them? Or her? Or did it just not care?

Time to think about it later. Pickett resumed swimming toward the back of the bar, where the open water could at least offer her air. When a pale stretch of moonlit water came into view, she kicked all the harder, pushing her poor protesting lungs until, at last, she broke through the surface.

Warm, smelly swamp air had never tasted so good. Pickett sucked in lungful after lungful of air, bobbing up and down in the water. And if the occasional gulp of grimy water filled her mouth, well, that wasn't the worst that had happened.

She coughed and kicked until she reached the boardwalk, grasping onto the old wood as her mind spun from the sudden influx of air. A hammer pounded inside of her head between her temples. She had to force her eyes to stay open, just enough to really pay attention to everything around her.

Dead things kept bobbing up to the surface. One turtle bumped by her leg, placid as a well-fed pig. Until its head breached the surface. Then, it let out a vicious hiss and snapped at her.

Pickett punched it back down, and it swam away as though it hadn't just been smacked by a giant.

What the actual fuck?

Pickett frowned, but this was her best shot. She sucked in a deep breath and pushed down into the water, holding on to the slimy wooden boardwalk supports. And sure enough, the dead moved through the water, methodical and detached. Just as with the swamp beast, the living wildlife followed them, nibbling and shoving, and the dead didn't seem to care or notice as they followed a trek up to the water, after which point they swamp back down, down, down to the deep dark of the swamp.

She pushed up, stealing one more gulp of air before she

swam down, following the path of the dead. As the dark and cold of the deep swamp began to wrap around her, a strange noise pierced through the dull roar of the underwater world.

It sounded like whispers and cries, as if someone moaned and weeped. Pickett kicked lower, and the whispers, just as breathy and heart wrenching, filled her mind. Strange grass grew like mold off the side of the slimy struts, swaying in the gentle currents. It glowed like it was basked in moonlight, even this far beneath the surface.

Pickett kicked closer, and the sounds of whispers and wails grew louder. Was she crazy, or was it the same color and thickness of the little mossy strands she'd found in Letterboy's finger? Pickett reached out and touched it. The strands felt like hair. She almost sucked in a lungful of water at the sudden vibrating pulse that made her feel her chest would explode. She wanted to wail. She wanted to scream. She wanted to curl up into a ball and never leave again, because nothing could ever heal the fractures in her heart.

Pickett pulled back, ripping a clump of grass free from the strut. The emotion softened, fading into a dull ache as the glowing grass went dark.

Heartbreak.

That's what Hoag had said. Heartbreak and sorrow. This is what had poisoned the swamp. Whatever magic this was, she had no idea. But if anyone might have a good idea, it would be him.

Pickett shoved the grass in her pocket and kicked up to the surface, punching a few fish, both living and dead, out of her way. As she hauled herself, dripping and filthy, up onto the boardwalk, a water snake tried to follow, but Pickett kicked it back. All right. She needed to get to Hoag.

But first, she needed to get those bastards out of her bar.

SEVENTEEN

Pickett wasn't as large as any of her attackers, and she probably wasn't smarter than at least one of them. But she'd bet fair coin that she had, in fact, more balls than all of them combined. Sometimes that was all it took to get something done.

Pickett leaned over, waiting until a handful of dead minnows joined the cycle heading up to the surface, then plucked them out of the water. It didn't take much to convince them to bite onto her hair, flapping violently and slapping her cheeks with her slimy tails. She draped a little swamp grass over her shoulder and smeared some mud on her face just for effect before she kicked open the back door to the kitchen.

As she left the kitchen and entered the main bar area, whatever scene she'd just barged in on came to an abrupt and horrifying stop. Five pairs of eyes locked onto her with varying degrees of revulsion. The bounty hunter had his fists up, but they wavered as his mouth fell open. Edie hugged Letterboy close, her brows furrowed. Slurne, predictably, rose to the top. He didn't soil himself, possibly because there was nothing left in his bowels to empty, but one look at Pickett and he began staggering back, whimpering and grasping behind him for a chair. Deggir just fucked off. One look at her, and he tossed the chairs holding the table over the front door, rolled the table out of the way, and charged onto the boardwalk. Pickett hoped the dead swamp beast got him.

Slurne kept the drama going, his eyes flooding with tears as he held the chair out in front of him like a shield.

"Pickett," he blubbered. "We panicked. We didn't mean to—"

Pickett raised one arm, and she didn't have to try too hard to make it shake with appropriate menace as she reached deep inside of her to croak out her most guttural moan.

"Get. Out."

Slurne dropped the chair, breaking one of the legs as he staggered back and turned, scrambling out of the door. With any luck, the swamp beast would eat very well that night indeed.

Pickett narrowed her eyes and turned, angling her shaking finger at the bounty hunter.

"You—"

"Give it up, Pickett," Edie cut in.

Pickett didn't lower her arm, but she did scale back on the menacing glower as she turned to Edie who stood, pinning a terrified Letterboy against her as she regarded Pickett the way a farmwife might regard a dog traipsing inside covered with shit.

"And get those things out of your hair," Edie added with a scowl. "You're going to stink."

"I just took a dip in the swamp; I already stink." But Pickett did as she was told, plucking the vicious little beasts out of her thick curls before they could burrow deeper. Letterboy stared at her with wide, teary eyes as he reached up, squeezing one of Edie's hands tightly.

Pickett sighed. "It's all right, kid. I survived."

"How?" he squeaked.

"I'll second that question." The bounty hunter crossed his arms.

Pickett glared at him. "Disappointed are you?"

"Pickett, he's not responsible," Edie insisted. "In fact, he stopped Slurne and the other guy from trying to throw me out too."

Yeah well, Pickett hadn't been around to see it so she wasn't too interested in extending gratitude to this guy.

"Had to sacrifice my cape," Pickett said, crossing her arms. "But under the water, those things don't give a shit about us."

"You mean they didn't attack you?" Edie frowned at that, but loosened her grip on Letterboy. Not that he let go of her hand.

Pickett headed to the bar, digging around for any surviving rum. All they had was a pitcher of bibblewood juice. At least the sour flavor would be sure to wake her up. She poured some directly into her mouth and grimaced, as it burned into her nose and singed the tip of her tongue. The headache tried to come back with a vengeance, making her eyes water.

"They attacked once I was out of the water." She coughed. "But if I smacked them back down, they stopped. It's like no magic I've ever seen."

"And exactly how much magic have you seen?"

Pickett was tempted to hurl the pitcher at the bounty hunter, but it would only waste juice, which she'd have to pay to replace.

"Remind me why you're still here?"

The bounty hunter looped his thumbs in his belt. "I came here to take down a dangerous man and get paid well to do it. But it looks like you two took care of it. And then some." He gestured at the bucket in the back corner. If Pickett peered closely, she could just make out the quivering of something moving inside.

"Apologies. Clearly I should have just let him slaughter me on his way out of the water."

The hunter took a step toward her. Pickett tightened her grip on the pitcher handle.

"I could always turn you in." He threatened. "The magical murderer. Or"—he tilted his head to the side, right in Edie's direction—"perhaps your accomplice?"

Pickett ground her teeth. "I thought you'd decided Marnoc was a bad man."

"Sure, but a bounty hunter's got to eat."

Pickett could do it. She could try, at least. She could smash the pitcher into the side of his head. But her own head ached, and even she knew it was a losing bet to pit her against someone larger, stronger, and certainly fresher than her. And if he was angry enough? It wasn't Pickett alone in this place with him.

Fuck it. She was going to lose the bar, anyway, but until Fistic came and took it from her, this was her home. Pickett clenched her jaw and reached below, pulling a full rum bottle from behind the bar and slamming it down between them. It was almost all they had left. There would be no repairs. No next payment. No bar. But they'd be alive.

"Pickett, this isn't the time," Edie hissed, but Pickett ignored her, sliding the bottle toward him.

The bounty hunter arched a brow. "For my troubles?"

"You stay here," Pickett instructed. "I'm paying you to guard the place in what I have left. If the bar's still standing when our rum boy comes back, I'll give you another."

A whole bottle of rum just to sit around in the safety of the Pick's Pocket. The bounty hunter glanced again at Edie, then nodded in understanding before he grasped the neck of the bottle.

"I'll keep the place safe."

Letterboy stepped closer to him. The bounty hunter frowned but rested a hand on his head. "The child too."

"Are you out of your mind?" Edie demanded. "Why do we even need him to look after the bar?"

"Because, there's someone else we need to go see." Pickett pulled some of the swamp grass out of her pocket. Out of the water, it looked just as slimy and dead as any other lump of vegetation, but just touching it made her chest tighten. If Hoag could taste the emotion in the water, then maybe he could explain how patches of underwater grass could whisper and mourn. If they knew that, then maybe they could stop it. "We may just be able to figure all of this out after all."

EIGHTEEN

Pickett changed into some dry clothes, but with only one pair of boots, each step brought more water squelching up around her soles. The waters continued to churn around them as the dead tried to rise.

"If one comes at you, just kick it back into the water." Pickett demonstrated by finding a turtle and punting it like a rogue ball. It let out a snarl as it sailed through the air, but did not surface again. "They just keep swimming up and down, so it'll buy us a few minutes until they swim back up to the surface."

Edie wrinkled her nose, but nodded as she followed, hitching up her pink skirt and kicking at the stray fish with her tattered shoe. The air between them felt as heavy as it was quiet. Relatively quiet since there was only so quiet a swamp could be with the dead splashing out of the water while the birds and frogs and bugs screeched their nightly serenades. It was like trying to have a quiet conversation in the Spotted Dick. At least there, most of the noise had come from people enjoying themselves. This was just miserable.

"Listen, Edie." Pickett tried to sort through all the things she wanted to say, the things she needed to say, and the things that might not piss Edie off even more. There wasn't much overlap. She cleared her throat and tried again. "Edie, you have to understand, the whole situation with Fistic started before you arrived." She glanced over at her shoulder, but Edie seemed to intentionally shift her gaze anywhere but at Pickett.

Pickett took a deep breath. "I didn't have a lot of prospects so I saw this old fishing shack and thought, 'Hey. Loads of people have to travel the swamps. Maybe they'd like to buy a drink. And how hard could it be to sling booze, right?' Only I didn't realize the shack needed repairs. Then it needed more. And I needed money. And then it was too late to get out of it."

"You could have run."

"I'd be running from the only thing that was ever mine," Pickett said grimly. "Besides, Fistic is a powerful man. If he doesn't get his coin back the usual way, then he's been known to take out indentured contracts on his borrowers. If I piss him off, gods know who he'd sell me to in order to earn his profits back. I could be gone for years. I might never make it back."

"Right," Edie muttered, and there came a loud plopping sound as she must have kicked a particularly fat creature back into the water. "And I was just supposed to find out one day when an enforcer came to drag you off?"

Pickett winced. "For what it's worth, I wasn't trying to hide it. Obviously, you saw how rotten the condition of the bar was."

"I did," Edie said tartly. "I saw. And I asked you again and again if we had money troubles, and every time you tried to distract me or tell me that everything was fine."

"Well, yeah." Pickett paused and turned to face her. "You showed up in the middle of the night with some madman after you, then you shared your fucking depressing life story. So you know what didn't occur to me? That an orphan milkmaid who'd had to commit a murder to escape harassment really needed money problems on top of-yeeouch!"

Pickett jumped a full foot in the air as something snapped

onto her already wounded ankle, sending blood seeping through the bandages. Without stopping to look, she kicked and sent the singular head of a hefty water snake flying back into the swamp.

"Serves you right!" Edie jumped as a nasty frog made for her and shoved it away as she crossed her arms. "And for the record, Pickett, that orphan milkmaid wound up having money problems she didn't know about."

"My problems are not your problems."

"They are when your home is my home," Edie snapped. "And here I am, primed to lose that same home, because I decided to trust the madwoman who thought scaring everyone off with the threat of magic she didn't have was going to solve everything."

"Not everything." Pickett gasped. "I'm not a complete imbecile."

"You could have fooled me." Edie glowered at her. "So what was the plan to pay back your lender?"

"I was working on it." Pickett threw her hands up in the air. "I thought I'd be able to handle it and you'd never have to find out."

Edie clenched her jaw. Her pale cheeks flooded with red as she hunched over. And as she began to stalk forward, Pickett had the sudden very real fear that she was about to be slapped. But Edie only shoved her shoulder as she stalked past her, right toward a particularly bulbous water lizard. With a growl, she kicked the thing so hard it split in two, sending dead guts sprinkling across the surface of the water.

"That's worse!" she shouted.

Pickett blinked. "How is that worse? I was protecting you."

"You were shutting me out." Edie angled a finger at her, her eyes burning despite the unshed tears that glossed over them. "My whole life I never had any control. I was a bad omen and I was told I was lucky to live in the barn and wear secondhand clothes. I thought when I started working for you that I was a part of something. That I was your partner."

"You were," Pickett said, but she couldn't really put any heat behind the words.

Edie shook her head. "You don't keep your partners in the dark like that." She bit her cheek and turned away. "Now can you please just show me where the hell this friend of yours is?"

Pickett's mouth bobbed open a few times, until she finally shut it and nodded. Right now, there was nothing she could say that would actually land outside of the "piss Edie off" category, so what did it really matter?

Maybe. Maybe not. Pickett's insides wriggled and, suddenly, she didn't want them to die with things this murky between them.

"You *were* my partner," Pickett said. "I've just had partners before. And it hadn't worked out."

"Because you couldn't trust them?" Edie bit, and Pickett's stomach dropped.

"No." She swallowed. "Because I trusted him too much. Kind of made me forget how to do it." She pointed down the boardwalk. "Hoag's boat should be just ahead," she said quietly, taking the lead. "Hoag's boat is . . ."

But there was no Hoag's boat. Usually she could see the large cabin and the useless mast from here, all that stretched ahead were the dark, roiling waters. Had he sailed off? No, he would never leave. Cold dread flooded her, and she rushed down the boardwalks, dodging and jumping over the stinking dead things that tried to clamber up. And, as she did, she saw the first remnants of the damage.

A skeleton missing an arm struggled in the ropey loops of an old net.

Fish attacked the wooden jellyfish, which looked less like its inspiration and more like a wooden sculpture of shit with each errant bite.

Ladles and buckets and all the flotsam of an eccentric life spread out in the swamp, carried away from the wreckage of what had once been Hoag's boat. The mast was gone. The cabin had been ripped open. The stern dipped underwater as dead things clambered onto it, snarling and snapping and hissing in search of something they weren't finding.

Edie gasped behind her. Pickett plowed forward, plucking a floating plank of wood as she jumped onto the boat.

"Hoag?" she shouted, whacking away lizards and fish and turtles and frogs and the foul remains of what must have been a stork pecking away at the planks of the deck. She tried to push her way into the cabin, put a dead woman wailed up at her, teeth gnashing as she tried to grab at Pickett's legs.

Pickett swung at her hands so hard they snapped off with a pop and snap of bone and skin and sinew.

"Pickett!" Edie shouted.

But Pickett ignored her. *Was Hoag in there? Was he drowned? Was he dead?*

She swung at the dead woman again and again, but she couldn't shove her back into the water. The hull of the boat must have been too intact for that trick to work. She smashed the creature's head in, splattering bits of brain and decaying bone onto the walls and tried to peer in past her. "Hoag!"

The creature screeched and threw herself forward to grasp Pickett's knee, pulling her down to the ground. Swamp water and mud soaked through her clothes as the plank flew from her hands and two amputated forearms punched into her gut again and again. Pickett wheezed and tried to roll out of the way, but she couldn't get enough of a grip on the slick deck.

Hands looped under her armpits, dragging her away just enough to enrage the creature. Pickett sucked in a deep breath and reached for Edie, holding her tight as she scrambled to her feet and dove for the boardwalk.

The creature snarled behind her and kept hurling herself up out of the cabin, but without hands to grip, she just kept sinking back down as the boat itself slipped lower and lower into the swamp.

"Your friend." Edie glanced down, her brows furrowed. But they both knew. Pickett sat up and stared at the debris littering the water. Among it all was an ugly little stuffed bunny. With a heavy heart, she lifted it out of the swamp, giving it a squeeze to wring out the water. For the life of her she'd never know why he cared so much about this ugly little thing. But he did.

She could almost imagine what he'd have said if he'd somehow still been around to see them.

"Oy there!"

Wait a minute. That wasn't her imagination. Pickett turned to see Hoag headed toward her, half in and half out of the water, lounging on the back of a massive, living swamp beast.

NINETEEN

The swamp beast swam forward, bumping its snout up against the boardwalk. Pickett scrambled to her feet and glanced around, but the wooden plank she'd used against the dead woman had already floated out into the roiling water. Out of reach. Not that she needed it, as it turned out.

Hoag swam up to the boardwalk, hauling himself up. The swamp beast sat placidly next to him, unperturbed at the dead things bobbing up and snarling around it.

"Hoag!" Pickett jumped forward, pulling the old man into a tight, albeit wet, hug. He grunted, patting the top of her head.

"Muriel needed me. Hope you weren't scared."

"Me?" Pickett stepped back, gesturing at the destruction of the house boat. "I thought you were dead? Why aren't you scared?"

"Oh, I have Muriel." He knelt down, patting the beast on the top of her head. She let out a soft rumble, blinking slowly. "My boat started rocking. Things came bursting through filled with sorrow and pain. I had a whole basket of biscuits and they soaked them. But I had to focus on her more. The dreadful things were after her nest."

"You-you abandoned your home to save a swamp beast's nest?"

Hoag drew back, pressing a hand to his chest. "Wrong! Wrong! You say beast with such disdain."

Muriel groaned softly in the water. Edie took a tentative step forward and knelt. "Is this . . Is she an armored lizard?" she asked. "I read about them."

Hoag gripped her arms. "You live in her realm. You must respect her as a matriarch of these waters. No mere beast. She is *the* beast. She's what armored lizards dream they used to be thousands of years ago, before they became the puppies they are today."

Right. They were, after all, speaking to Hoag. Edie awkwardly extricated herself from his grasp. Pickett cleared her throat and tried to imagine herself back on his boat, asking for insane advice. She straightened and held the bunny out, just to show that she was, in fact, holding it.

"Right. Well uh, is *the* beast's nest all right?"

He closed his eyes and inclined his head, not even glancing over to kick a fish that jumped up to bite him.

"It was a near thing. She smelled the worst of it all. Her nest was right in the sorrow, where it was quiet and poisoned. We were lucky. Her whole clutch survived. Each egg accounted for."

Great. More of her spiky, toothy ilk swarming around the swamp. But surely it wouldn't be any worse than what was happening now.

"Hoag, we need help." She gripped the front of his shirt, pulling some of the moss from her pocket. "I think I've figured something out."

Hoag grunted at it, eyes narrowing before he glanced over at Edie and grunted. Pickett cleared her throat and held the bunny out to her.

"What are you doing?" Edie whispered.

"Just take it."

"I don't want it."

"He won't help if you don't hold the bunny."

"You're already holding it."

Pickett shot Edie a sharp look. Edie scowled but, finally, took the bunny.

Hoag nodded solemnly and held the swamp grass up, running his fingers over each wet little curl. Muriel rumbled behind him, knocking back the dead trying to rise up with her massive tail. After a long moment, he gave it a sniff, then nibbled on the edge of it. Pickett bit back her disgust at the sight.

After chewing it thoughtfully, he spat it back into the swamp, then dropped the wad of swamp grass at his feet, hopping around it once, twice, three times. Then, he hopped again in the opposite direction before nudging it into the water.

"Where'd you say you found it?"

"Growing down in the swamp below Pick's Pocket."

Hoag grunted and eased himself down, picking at his toes thoughtfully. Edie shot Pickett a wide-eyed look, which Pickett refused to return.

"This shouldn't be there," he said. "This moss doesn't grow this far south and it's not known to like water."

Pickett frowned. "I found it all over some rocks."

"That all you find?"

"Whispers." She crossed her arms. "The closer I got to it, the more I heard whispers. I couldn't make out what they were saying but they sounded sad."

Hoag grunted for them to sit. Pickett hesitated, glancing back at the ruins of the boat, but for the moment the dead on that side of the boardwalk seemed far more interested in the wreckage than in the humans nearby. She sat down.

Hoag shot Edie a steely look until, with a grimace, she followed suit, tucking her skirt around her knees.

"That grass," Hoag said, pointing a knobby finger at the water, "is the sorrow poisoning the water."

Shit. And they'd pulled some of it out of Letterboy's finger. Would it have killed him too? What about anyone else bitten by one of the undead who might have some tangled up in their teeth? Pickett didn't have the nerve to look at her own bitten ankle. She'd deal with it later.

"How did it get here?" Edie asked.

Hoag stared at her for a long moment, then leaned forward. Edie leaned back, but he only pressed his ear to the bunny. After a long moment, he nodded and straightened.

"It rode here in a pocket," he said solemnly. "And it whispers sorrow and longing into the waters. This is the source of the poison."

"So it was introduced to the swamps?" Edie pressed. "Like an infestation."

But Hoag only shook his head. "No, this is being sustained by whispers."

"Hang on." Pickett held up her hand. "I thought you said those sounds were coming from the swamp grass."

Hoag shot her a blank look. "I did, yes, but the grass gets it from somewhere else. Grass can't talk, even to sorcerers."

Pickett's cheeks began to burn. Well, how was she supposed to know that? After everything she'd seen, nothing seemed strange anymore.

"Makes sense, I suppose. What is it saying?" Edie asked.

Hoag peered at her, then scooted to her side. "Are you a sorceress as well?"

"Uh, I . . ." Edie shot Pickett a look.

Pickett shrugged. "If you like, sure."

Hoag glanced between them. Then, with a decisive nod, he thumped a fist against his chest.

"The grass whispers of necromancy, trying to revive what should have died. But death and grief? Those are poisons too.

The moss's maker is spilling that poison into everything they touch." His expression grew uncharacteristically solemn. "It seeks the dead. The dead seek life they cannot taste. They will kill because that is the only thing this magic remembers. Death and sorrow."

Edie wrinkled her nose. "And if this sorrow gets into some-one's food?"

Hoag patted his stomach. "The body won't take it. This magic isn't for the living. The living can't take it in."

"Hence the swamp crab stew," Pickett muttered. This stood to get so much worse. If the dead kept on killing, then there might be nothing safe left for people to eat. Suppose this sorrow and grass and all the dead swam out further into the waterways leading into Southfen? To the ocean? "These whispers could destroy everything."

"All right, well what is it actually saying?" Edie wanted more. "The whispers. If we know the specifics maybe we can get to the bottom of it."

Hoag shrugged. "Oh, I dunno. I don't speak Northish languages."

"Andoshi," Pickett corrected, then her brain kicked in. "Son of a dog and a penny-pip whore!" She jumped to her feet and towered over Hoag. "You're sure? You're absolutely positive the grass is speaking something Andoshi? Northish?"

"It's whispering," Hoag said, squirming a little under her stare. "Not disrespecting a sorceress or nothing."

Edie inhaled, then exhaled slowly through her nose before resting a hand on Hoag's shoulder. "There's no disrespect. Everybody here is a friend." She glanced down at the bunny in her hand, then set it on his knee. "What Pickett's asking is, are you sure that's the language it's whispering in?"

Hoag regarded her as though she'd just asked the question directly from her ass.

"It's whispering," he repeated. "It's Northish because it's

whispering. North magic is the whispers. Nobody much knows how it works, just how it sounds." He narrowed his eyes and glanced up at Pickett. "Hold on. How do you not know that?"

Pickett planted her hands on her hips and puffed out her chest. "Specialization."

For the first time that night, she had a vague idea of what she might be able to do. She knew who was at the heart of it. How many other Northish people did she know? Particularly Andoshi people with a penchant for whispering to themselves, who looked at an undead fish like it was pure gold. How many other looney old men conveniently disappeared right before everything went to shit?

The Northfellow wasn't a bad sort. He was just old. And a little out of his mind. Fuck. Just a few days ago he'd been drunk and spewing about love and heartbreak, hadn't he? The answers to everything had been right in front of her and she'd clammed up when she should have responded to it. But it might not be too late. Maybe if she could just talk to him, perhaps scare him a little, he'd undo whatever he'd done. They could fix the swamp, then they could worry about scrounging together the money they needed. Once word got out that the swamp witch had saved everyone, they might be financially grateful.

Edie, on the other hand, looked crestfallen. "It can't be," she insisted. "You don't honestly believe it's the Northfellow?"

"Grief can make people do crazy things." She crouched down next to Hoag. "Do you think you can track the heart of these whispers?"

Hoag blinked owlishly at her, then burst out laughing.

"Fuck no. I'm just a crazy old coot. I'm no sorcerer." He jabbed a finger toward the swamp beast. "But I think my friend can help you."

CHAPTER

TWENTY

Pickett had been through many strange experiences in her life, but nothing like this. With the dead writhing around her, it was all she could do to hold on for dear life to the rope Hoag had handed her. The rope he'd knotted carefully and looped around his swamp beast's chest, kicking through the murky water as they followed her steady trek to wherever the scent of death was strongest. Inside the water, the dead could be kicked off easily enough. As for everything else in the swamp that could kill them, it paid to have a literal swamp beast as a friend.

For her part, Edie looked vaguely green in the pale moonlight. But she held on tight to her loop of rope, enough though her bony knuckles popped up like stones from her thin hand. Pickett wanted to reach over and squeeze her wrist, but she didn't dare let go of her own handhold. Even as the sweeping of Muriel's tail kept splashing muddy water into her face.

They were heading into the heart of whatever this strange swamp infection was.

The thought of the Northfellow, her loyal regular, being

147

behind all of this made Pickett's heart tighten. He never much struck her as a malicious person. Quite the opposite. Clearly, she'd fallen into the trap of judging a whorehouse by its paint job. And what a filthy and wretched whorehouse it apparently was.

"What will we do when we find him?" Edie yelled over the splashing of the swamp beast.

"What?" Pickett glanced at her, dread pooling in her stomach.

No, she couldn't be considering it. But Edie's face was set, her lower jaw jutting out. Gentle, sweet Edie who gave her last coin to send Letterboy to the surgeon was the same woman who'd killed Marnoc and dumped his body in the swamp. Edie would do whatever it took to survive.

"We have to be ready to finish the job," Edie called.

There it was. Whatever it took. It was one thing to fight off a monster chasing a girl into her bar. It was something else to do any of that to a sweet old man. Is that what Edie was prepared to do? Had she given up on herself that much in this one awful night?

"Edie—" she called, but before she could find the words, a rotten fish tail slapped her in the face, leaving her sputtering and gagging. She gripped the rope tighter and glanced around, prepared to smack the next one out of the way. There weren't any more though. Strange. It seemed the further they went, the fewer dead there were roiling in the waters. Were they spreading out, pushing away from this mysterious source? Or was there a protective barrier in the magic itself?

They slowed as they began to push through thick grasses leading to a muddy bank. Through the tall grass, Pickett thought she spotted a light from a window in the near distance. When Muriel slowed down and turned parallel to the shore, Pickett took the hint and dismounted. She squelched through the mud, swaying back and forth as she tried to keep her balance, until she reached relatively solid ground. Edie clutched her shoes in one hand, her expression resolute.

"Um, thank you," Pickett said, glancing back at the beast. Muriel grunted and backtracked, her golden eyes trained on Pickett until she sank back down into the water. There went their ride out of here.

As far as Pickett knew, there were no settlements on this side of the swamp. Just stretches of mud and grass and frogs and snakes. And apparently swamp beasts. Maybe that was a good thing. There was really no telling for sure how this thing would affect a full settlement. Of course it did beg the question of how the Northfellow got to this isolated location.

Edie didn't even look down as she pulled her shoes back on and plowed ahead, making for the distant light that had to be the Northfellow's house.

"I don't see anything living around here," Pickett muttered. The night air, usually warm, felt suddenly chilly against her damp skin and she shivered.

Edie glanced back. "It makes sense, doesn't it?" She kicked a spitting, snarling turtle out of the way. "The wounds they inflict don't heal and they attack without reason. They might have killed half the creatures that come to land by this point."

And it would only be a matter of time until there was no life left.

"If that bounty hunter has any sense, he'll take Letterboy and make for Southfen. Try and get ahead of this curse."

"It won't do any good if this gets into the rivers," Edie said grimly. "If we want to have any sort of home, then we've got to cut it off here."

She had that look on her face again. The one that chilled Pickett right to the bone.

"Edie, you never said what you were planning to do."

Edie stopped and turned, sinking a little into the thick mud that sucked at their feet.

"I'm going to do *something*!" she hissed.

"What does that even mean?"

"I'm not having this argument now," Edie snapped. "And when we get back to the bar, I'm not going to sit in the back and follow your lead anymore."

"Edie . . ." And what could she say? That they might not make it through the night to go home anyway? That Fistic might still take it from them? He didn't even need the excuse of her not being able to pay anymore. They'd killed his enforcer. That was as screwed as they got. But saying so now would just be ripping the scab off an unhealed wound.

"We can't kill him," she said instead. "He's just a sad old man."

"Then we'd better hope we can find a better option." Edie turned, dragging her feet out of the muck to continue her long, ponderous trek toward the light.

Hunched over the water, his beard gone brown from the mud, the Northfellow looked even more insane than usual. It didn't help that he was talking, no, whispering into the waters. Just a few feet behind him, the light shone from what must have been his house. It made the Pick's Pocket look like a tasteful villa. The whole structure was made of vines and sticks and logs, not so much assembled as cobbled together into a clumsy hut that probably kept the rain out. It might have been a random pile of swamp debris were it not for the lantern light glowing from within the windows.

Pickett gave Edie's shoulder a squeeze. "Let me talk to him."

"Pickett—"

"Hey." Pickett gestured at the waters. "We haven't been so much as nipped since we got here. I think it'll be safe. Just let me try."

"And if it doesn't go well?"

Pickett sighed. "Then I won't stop you."

Edie clenched her jaw but nodded. "Don't die."

"Back at you." Pickett tried to smile, but the effort only made her feel queasy, so she quickly abandoned it as she pulled away, slogging to the muck where her old regular sat hunched over. Pickett hesitated, then rested a hand on his shoulder.

"Hello there," she whispered. "You're looking crazier than usual, old man."

The Northfellow blinked, then raised his chin. His eyes had the bright, glazed look of a man caught in a fever.

Pickett squeezed his shoulder. "Yeah. It's me. Listen. What you're doing. It's got to stop."

"What I'm doing . . ." He wheezed, then blinked. "I'm bringing him back."

"What, the stupid fish?" Pickett snapped. "You're going to kill the whole swamp."

"No," the Northfellow wheezed, shaking his head. "No, I'm bringing *him* back."

And with that, he shoved his head in the water, breathing out a few fat air bubbles.

"Oldam's rocky nosehairs!" Pickett hissed, lunging forward to grasp the back of his shirt and yank him up out of the water.

The Northfellow whimpered and wriggled against her grasp, coughing and clawing at the water. "No," he keened, jerking away from Pickett's grasp to hurl himself into the swamp, swimming feebly out.

Shit! Picked scrambled to her feet and started to wade in after him, but the reeking mud had no sooner begun to seep into her shoes than she stopped, her chest tightening. She could go after him. She could drag him back. Or she could just let him go. If she did, Edie wouldn't feel the need to—

No. Fuck. That wasn't right. Edie was definitely smarter than she was. So if the decision here really was to let that looney old coot off himself and potentially take the curse with him, it wasn't a decision she was going to make on her own.

Oh. That was it, was it? Edie wasn't like anyone else Pickett had ever known or loved. There was no guarantee she was going to ditch when things got hard. And she'd already murdered two people, albeit in self-defense. Why the good fuck was Pickett so desperate to protect her virtue?

Perhaps this wasn't the moment for a revelation like this, what with the Northfellow swimming out facedown into the swamp. But that more or less tracked for her.

"Edie!" she called, turning to squelch her way right back out of the swamp. "Edie, I could use your help!"

"And I could use yours!" Edie pushed aside the ratty cloth that passed for a door in the wretched hut. "I think I found whatever he's been using."

She held out what looked like a bone. And maybe it was morbid of her to think it, but it looked kind of like a human bone, though the last thing she wanted to do was guess where it had come from. Especially given that it looked like it had dozens of strange symbols, maybe runes or letters, carved into it along with strange wrappings in varying shades of blue. Pickett wrinkled her nose and jerked a thumb behind her. "So . . . the Northfellow threw himself into the swamp."

Edie's expression fell. She clenched the bone to her chest. "Is that, I mean, is that going to fix this?"

"Guess that depends on how well he can swim."

Pickett glanced over to see fresh bubbles billowing up from the swamp. And, perhaps, growing closer?

An elderly head broke through the water, his wide, feverish eyes fixed on them as he sucked in several sharp breaths. Pickett took a step back, but it didn't spare her ears from his desperate scream.

"No! Put it back!"

Huh?

Pickett turned back to Edie, but the first thing she saw was the bone. The massive, awful, maybe-human bone, its yellow-gray color darkening as it vibrated in Edie's fingers. Edie screeched and leaped back, dropping the bone to the ground, but it was too late. Cracks splintered the surface as the bone turned black and, little by little, crumbled like burnt wood in the air.

"No!" the Northfellow screeched as he squelched past the swamp grasses onto the shore, rushing past Pickett and toward his shack.

It didn't take long for Pickett to guess why. She glanced over her shoulder and saw the dark of the swamp waters, dark and still. Then a bubble appeared at the surface. It burst, and, like a belch, filled the air with the familiar, noxious swamp stench. But there was more to it. More than the usual smell of decay, it had an odor of death.

Pickett's heart skipped a beat. She took a step back.

More bubbles rose to the surface. Then the water began to churn. Something was moving beneath the surface.

"Gods." Edie breathed.

The churning turned to roiling splashes of white breaking through the dark as deadened hands and fins and legs cut through the surface. Whatever protection they'd had from the dead, it was gone.

"Oh, come on!" Pickett shouted, and the stupid part of her wanted to grab a rock and hurl it at the nearest dead thing, but hands closed around her arm, jerking her back before she could give in to any idiotic instinct.

"This way," Edie hissed, and Pickett didn't even bother trying to fight it. After all, Edie was smarter than her, time to follow her lead.

She yanked her feet free of the mud and turned, squelching

and squeaking through the swampy shore to the poor shelter of the Northfellow.

"I hope this pile of debris can keep us safe," she cried.

"Well," Edie called. "We only need one of us to tell the story."

Then she dove through the shack's narrow cloth. And all Pickett knew to do was follow her.

TWENTY-ONE

ar the door!" Edie shouted, which was a generous descriptor for the cloth that hung in the front of the hut and an even more optimistic take on their resources. There was a bedroll, an old crate with a bunch of junk in it, and that was about it.

"Shit, shit, shit!" Pickett hissed, whirling around, in search of anything they could use when something cold and wet tangled into her hair, yanking her back.

"Edie!" she cried, and in an instant Edie was there, yanking a stick from the "wall" of the shelter and bringing it down hard on a very dead, very human arm. It snapped off with a pop and the sudden stench of rotting meat.

Edie grabbed her arm, yanking her back a second before the ramshackle wall began to shudder.

"Guess that was a load-bearing stick," Pickett said. Since there was no getting out of it, she grabbed one of her own, brandishing it in preparation. The ceiling creaked, then gave as half the hut slid down, collapsing into the doorway and leaving their heads exposed.

The Northfellow sat in the middle of all of it, knees on the dirt as he rocked back and forth, mumbling in Andoshi. So he was as helpful as a lead buoy.

Pickett backed up until she felt Edie bumping up against her shoulder blades.

"How much do you want to hope that there aren't too many dead human bodies around here?"

"Are you asking what I hope or what I think?"

Bodies clambered, making the wooden ring of what had once been a shelter shake. Pale hands grasped the sticks and vines at the top of the shelter. Pickett tightened her grip on her weapon and took a deep breath.

"Edie, if we don't make it through this—"

"Shut up, Pickett."

The Northfellow continued to rock and whimper, occasionally muttering "I didn't want this. I didn't want any of this."

The first dead face cleared the edge of the wooden barricade, its eye sockets empty and its lower jaw missing, yet it managed to continue hissing and snarling. And suddenly, Pickett hurt so much. Her feet still ached where she'd been nipped earlier. Her back and shoulders ached where she'd been knocked to the ground by the dead thing that used to be Marnoc. A chill stole over her, creeping from the linen of the shirt sticking to her skin right into her blood. For a brief, mad moment, she wondered how bad it would feel to die. Surely she wouldn't feel herself turning into one of those things if she wound up in the water. The only pity was that it was definitely going to hurt.

As Pickett raised her stick, the Northfellow lurched to his feet, eyes squeezed shut as he flung his arms out and, in a voice that echoed like a whole chorus, bellowed, "No!"

It wasn't sound, exactly, but it wasn't air that burst out of him, slamming into Pickett like a wave. Her feet flew out from under her. Her back hit the ground. Breath hissed out between her teeth as she stared, dazed and wide-eyed, up at the dead face peering down at them a second before it too was blown back.

The world went silent. Then like the first rays of dawn peeking over the horizon, a soft ringing pierced Pickett's ears. The Northfellow dropped to his knees, his bright eyes awash with tears. His beard waggled as he spoke, but even before the ringing faded enough for Pickett to hear his words, she could guess what he was saying.

"I'm sorry. I'm sorry. I'm sorry."

With a grunt, Pickett pushed herself into a sitting position. "Did you stop it?"

"What?" The Northfellow turned, a tear sliding down his craggy cheek.

"Did you stop it? Are the dead back to being dead?"

"No," he croaked. "They are just away from us. For a little while."

For a little while. Right. Hard to decide whether it was time to breathe a sigh of relief or brace herself for the inevitable.

"All right, well, fix it now, then."

"I-I can't," he whispered, dropping his face into his hands.

"Bukker's cock-rainbow, you can't," Pickett cried, scooting closer to him. "Listen. The dead are multiplying. Look at this." She tugged her shoe off, and with it pooled dark blood mixed with mud. She shoved his shoulder to get his attention. "Look at this! This wound came from a dead thing. This wound isn't going to heal. They all keep swimming over and over in circles and if they encounter anything above the water, they try to kill it. And they'll swim in circles over and over until every living thing in the swamp is dead!"

"Maybe not just the swamp." Edie scooted up next to her. "If this, whatever it is, is in the water, then it might spread to the rivers. To the oceans."

"So. No pressure but"—Pickett shoved him again with her bleeding foot—"we just need you to go ahead and save the world. Preferably before the dead come back."

"It's not supposed to . . . I can't. I'm so close." He shook his head. "This isn't what was supposed to happen."

"Well it is happening!" Pickett snapped, grabbing his shoulder. "Why did you keep this going after you saw that stupid fish? What are you getting out of this?"

He muttered something in Andoshi, then sagged against her, burying his face in the crook of her shoulder. Pickett stiffened as he sobbed, wrapping his arms around her middle. Poor, miserable old fuck. He needed someone who knew what to do here. All he got was her, patting his back and wishing desperately she knew what to say.

"It was years. I've tried for years. I thought I'd finally got it to work. I'm sorry. I had to make it right. I had to make it better."

Pickett stared at Edie, her heart pounding. If they couldn't talk sense into him . . .

Edie nodded back at her and reached out, squeezing his shoulder. Pickett squeezed her eyes shut. She didn't want to see what Edie was about to do, especially not when the Northfellow was pressed right up against her like this. But she wasn't prepared for Edie to begin speaking gently.

"It sounds like you regret something," she said. "You know, I can tell you a little about regret."

The Northfellow didn't budge, but his sobs grew a little quieter. As best as Pickett could guess, he was probably trying to quiet down so he could listen.

Polite lunatic.

"Growing up, I used to dream of a big life," Edie said gently. "The kind I knew I'd never have. Nobody knew where I came from so nobody trusted me. Even when I was a child. I milked cows and read anything I could get my hands on and dreamed of adventures and family and a house of my own."

Pickett's heart twinged. Of course, she knew all of this but hearing it again like this felt like a condemnation. A house and a family, all the things she hadn't been able to provide. Just danger and a bar and a drunk fraud who didn't listen. And yet, if those things were the closest Edie was going to get, then she was still going to lose it. Because Pickett wasn't clever enough to find a way out of this mess.

"I thought I found a way to get that though," Edie went on, rubbing her hand up and down the Northfellow's back. "A good man was willing to marry me. Neither of us was going to be suited for marriage in the traditional sense. We were going to be oddballs together. He'd have his lovers. I'd have a house. But it didn't work out that way."

Pickett's gut squirmed. She hated this story. She hated that one of the best things that had happened to her only happened because Edie had to suffer something awful. Why wasn't life as simple as getting to enjoy good things and good results?

"An awful man couldn't let me be happy," Edie continued. "He attacked the good man who was going to marry me. He killed his own brother. When he realized what he'd done, he blamed me for tempting him. I ran. He followed." Edie's hand stilled as she set her jaw. "I had to do something I swore I'd never do. Become someone I didn't want to become. I've tried to think of a thousand ways I could have avoided it. But I can't go back and change it."

She glanced up at Pickett with a sad smile, then turned back to the Northfellow. "What is it you're trying to make better with all of this?"

The Northfellow lifted his head slowly to stare at Edie with watery, red-rimmed eyes. Pickett rushed to scramble out of the way before he could go in for another hug.

Sniffing loudly as a little loose mucus still slipped out of his nose and into his beard, he shuddered and wiped at it haphazardly. "Rogr. His name was Rogr."

"Rogr," Edie repeated. "And you loved him?"

The Northfellow's face crumpled. He squeezed his eyes shut, nodding weakly as fresh tears flowed down his cheeks.

"I was supposed to be there. I was supposed to watch his back." He broke off into Andoshi, but Pickett could guess the gist of it all. Love. Loss. Regret. Insane plan to bring back the dead.

"Old man," Pickett said, leaning forward, albeit not enough for another hug. "You really think your Rogr would be all right with all of this happening?"

The Northfellow let out a whimper, then a wail as he rocked back and forth. Tears streamed down his craggy cheeks, pooling in his wrinkles for a moment before they slipped to the ground. He shook his head, his white hair dancing around him like clouds before he staggered out of the hut. Pickett should have been annoyed but she just felt . . . It was heavy in her chest. She didn't want to call it pity. She never wanted to act like she ever felt pity for anyone. Pity was the worst thing she could feel.

"I'll take care of him," she muttered.

"Careful," Edie mouthed, and Pickett nodded before slipping out a gap between walls.

The Northfellow sat in the shallows, just where the earth started to turn to mud. He sat like a stone, regardless of the cold or distant writhing of the dead near the surface. Pickett knew how it worked. Heartbreak had a strangely numbing effect.

She crept slowly into the muddy shallows, cringing at the feeling of the mud filling her shoes and sucking at her skin. And it stank like weeds and rot and, strangely, farts. But farts would not be enough to turn her back on a night like this.

She knelt next to the Northfellow. He didn't even glance her way. He just stared down at the muddy water like he could somehow see something powerful in it. And Pickett didn't even have to know magic to know that wasn't the case.

"Even if it somehow worked after all of"—Pickett gestured

vaguely at the world around them—"you know, this, he wouldn't be happy, would he?"

The Northfellow let out a soft whimper and rocked back and forth. More tears spilled down his cheeks, followed by a dribble of snot from his nose. But, after a second, his chin sagged down to his chest. It wasn't exactly a verbal affirmative, but it wasn't nothing either.

"Especially not since you did it without asking him first," she pointed out, scooting a little closer.

The Northfellow wiped his nose and glanced up. "Well…no. He is dead. I cannot ask."

"Exactly," Edie pressed. "So, if he comes back, it'll just be to this disaster. That wouldn't make him happy, would it?"

The Northfellow shook his head. "I wanted to make things right."

And the tremble in his voice. The way his beard shook as he raised his chin and stared at her. His red-rimmed eyes. Fuck, she pitied him, didn't she? Because she knew exactly how it felt to be lost. She knew how it felt to be desperate to do anything, try anything to take back a little bit of power and make the pain stop. Even if it meant buying a broken-down fishing shack in the middle of a swamp. But what he'd done had taken it way too far.

"You can still make this right for everyone else." Pickett rested a hand on his shoulder. "Please. Come back inside and tell us what to do, old man."

TWENTY-TWO

This was one of those moments Pickett wished she knew anything at all about magic. Because as he walked around in erratic patterns and muttered to himself, she had no way of knowing what was helpful and what was just whatever was wrong with him—senility or insanity or just the decaying influence of a lifetime of guilt. As he prepared to do whatever he was going to do, Pickett paced the perimeter of the hut, glancing through the odd gap in the wood. Dead things slumped in the mud and grass, little more than pale hunks of reeking meat, at least until they began to twitch. A hand here. A fin there. They didn't have a whole lot of time.

"So are we all ready to put them back to sleep or . . ."

"Sshh!" Edie hissed.

Pickett turned to see the Northfellow finally sinking down, legs crossed as he twined his fingers. Well half of them, with one set of fingers folded and the other set pointing straight up. He took a deep breath, then nodded.

"I was a soldier," he said slowly. Maybe because the words were important. Maybe just because he was trying to avoid slipping back into Northish. Either way, it felt right to sit down in front of him, hands on her knees. To be fair, there was a break in the hut she could glance through, with a dead turtle on its back she could eye for movement.

Edie nodded and leaned forward. "Yes? Go on."

Hard to believe she'd briefly been prepared to kill him.

The Northfellow squeezed his eyes shit.

"I was a soldier," he repeated. "In my country. We fought others of our country. And some hired from other places."

"You mean mercenaries?" Pickett couldn't help blurting.

Edie huffed and swatted Pickett's knee. "Not the time for a vocabulary lesson."

The Northfellow grimaced, then shook his head. "Rogr was my partner. We had love. But we also had a war to fight. We promised . . ." He took a shuddering breath. "We promised when it ended, we would be together. We would farm. We would serve. It did not matter. We would fight. We would live. Together. But I had to deliver a message."

Through the crack in the stick shelter, the dead turtle's clawed limb twitched violently. Enough to shake its whole body. Pickett's heart skipped a beat. How long until the dead humans rose? Was there a swamp beast among the dead?

A hand closed around hers, giving it a tight squeeze. Pickett sucked in a deep breath. For all she knew, the story was part of the ritual.

"I promised Rogr I would return," the Northfellow said, his chin dipping. "He had a knife. From his mother. It gave him luck. He gave it to me. I should not have taken it, but I did. I delivered my message. Enemies tried to kill me many times. They died. The knife saved and protected me. But when I returned, Rogr was dead. I had his knife. I lived. And he did not."

Despite herself, Pickett couldn't help squeezing Edie's hand back.

"That wasn't your fault," Edie insisted, but the Northfellow only shook his head.

"Many have lived lifetimes since he died. I promised him life. I could not give it."

"But he had a life, even if it was short." Edie shrugged. "You can't downplay how valuable the life he had was by focusing on all the time he didn't get. You knew him. Maybe just be glad for that."

Pickett's chest tightened and she nodded. "What she said."

The Northfellow gave a jerky nod and closed his eyes, pressing his hands to his chest. Softly, he began to whisper to himself, rocking back and forth, then front to back. The air shivered around them, shaking the sticks and branches of his house. Pickett squeezed Edie's hand tighter and braced herself.

The Northfellow slumped over like an emptied sack.

Pickett caught her breath and waited for . . . Well nothing in particular, it seemed.

"I guess that's it?" Edie glanced at Pickett. Pickett glanced at Edie, then extracted her hand and crept forward to press her fingers to his throat. His pulse was weak and thready, but he still seemed to be breathing.

"Hang on," she said, rolling him onto his back. "I think he's just out."

Edie crept to one of the holes in the wall of the hut and peeked out while Pickett shook his bedroll out and draped it over him.

"I think it worked," Edie announced. "Nothing's moving out there anymore."

Small reliefs.

Pickett patted the top of the bedroll with a sigh and leaned back on her haunches. "All right. Assuming the Pick's Pocket is still in one piece without us, I say we bring him with us in the morning. Give him a safe place to—"

He shuddered under the bedroll, his mouth falling open.

"Hey!" Pickett lunged forward, grasping his shoulders. "What's wrong, old man? Come on, what do you need?"

His mouth fell open and, with a low groan, he suddenly went utterly slack in her arms. No breath. No pulse.

No, this wasn't how it was supposed to work. They were supposed to save him so he could save the swamp. Not this. He wasn't supposed to die in the process. Pickett gave him a little shake, as though that might be enough to wake him. When it didn't, her cheeks began to burn.

"Stupid old coot," she whispered, and lay him back on the ground. He looked peaceful. Moreso than he ever had even in his deepest drunken stupor. Her eyes began to sting, and hot tears slid down her cheeks. "He didn't tell us."

Edie sank down next to her, staring down at him in silence. If she noticed the tears, she was polite enough not to mention them.

"He was in the bar every night," she murmured. "Until he wasn't."

"He was always a decent sort of man," Edie agreed.

"Do you think he knew what would happen if he stopped the spell?"

Edie's lips twitched. She began fiddling with a hole in her bodice. "I think it'll be nicer to decide that he did. It means he went out on his own terms. Sacrificing himself to save the swamp makes him kind of a hero."

Yeah. Maybe. Maybe.

"It's mad what a lonely person will do."

"Or a guilty person," Edie agreed, resting a hand on Pickett's shoulder. "Good thing we don't have to know what it's like."

Pickett let out a wet laugh and nodded.

CHAPTER

TWENTY-THREE

I t didn't take long for them to reject the possibility of dumping his body in the swamp. Even with the dead returning to their natural state, there'd been way too many human corpses out in those waters. It felt cheap to add another.

And, without shovels or hoes, a grave was out. If they tried, they'd only prolong the inevitability of something digging up the remains and making a lunch of him. Fortunately for them, he lived in a house of sticks, and it hadn't rained recently.

Pickett pulled the bedroll up over his face. It felt like the appropriate thing to do, even if it left his boots exposed. In another time, if she hadn't known him, Pickett might not have wanted to waste those boots. But sacrifices could be made. It wasn't like a new pair of too-large boots would somehow fix all of her problems.

As she and Edie worked to dismantle his hut and build what they assumed would be a decent pyre, they paused occasionally to gaze out into the waters. Hunks of the whispering moss floated to the surface, gray and dead and mercifully silent. All alongside bloody and dismembered fish, some guts, and various

166

other shapes she didn't particularly feel like identifying in that moment.

The actual issue of getting the pyre going, of course, was something entirely different. What Pickett wouldn't give in that moment for her flints. But they were at the bottom of the swamp around the bar now, and she probably wasn't going to get them back. Luckily for both of them, Edie read everything she could get her hands on, including stories that involved clever ways people got fires started when they had absolutely nothing useful on hand.

"This is taking forever," Pickett muttered as she continued sawing at one stick with another with as much strength as she had. Which, admittedly, wasn't much. It had been a very, very long night, and she wasn't particularly enthusiastic about the prospect of burning her friend's corpse. But there they were.

"Are you suggesting we leave him?" Edie grunted, glaring down at her own sticks as she rubbed them frantically.

"No," Pickett said, turning away. "Just stating facts."

"Could you state the facts once we finish?"

Much longer and her arms would be the only thing burning, but she kept at it. Of course, in the end she could have been as lazy as she wanted because it was Edie's sticks that began to smoke first. She tucked them into the pyre with some dried vines and leaves, blowing softly until the first sparks sent a warm glow spreading through the pile.

"Do all village girls know how to do that," Pickett asked, all too happy to throw hers on the fire.

Edie grinned. "Just the murderous foundling milkmaids."

Cheeky minx. "Oh, so we're joking about the killing now."

"I shudder to think what I'd do if I couldn't make myself laugh about it."

Yeah. Pickett understood that. The flames picked up, enveloping the Northfellow's body and flooding the air with blessed heat. Pickett shuddered as it chased some of the chill away and took a step forward, holding her palms up.

"Pickett!" Edie gasped. "Are you using a funeral pyre to warm up?"

"I'm cold," Pickett pointed out.

Edie stared at her for a long, scandalized moment. Then she too stepped forward, holding her hands out.

As the fire really caught, sending sparks flying up into the night sky, Pickett began to relax.

"He was my first customer, you know," she said. "When I first started. Couldn't quite convince anyone to come inside. They all thought it was a scam to rob them."

"It sort of is," Edie pointed out.

"They thought it was the sort of scam where there were no drinks and I held them at knife point. Or else they were trying to hold me at knife point, and I had to pretend I would hex their bloodline if they didn't back off. But him? He just stumbled in one day, sat at the bar, and asked for whatever I had. Just like that. He just came in and did business with me."

Edie dropped her hands and edged closer, looping her arm in Pickett's. "I like to think you gave him a safe place to come be with people. However lonely he was."

"We did. Together." Pickett raised her chin and watched the sparks dance up into the night. "Well, Rogr. Hope you give him a warm welcome."

"Excuse me," came a masculine, heavily accented voice. "How do you know my name?"

Pickett stiffened and, on her arm, Edie did, too. As one, they turned to see a youngish man, his beard tied into two short braids. He dressed in the far-outdated Northish fashion of ties and furs. Because of course he did. And of course Pickett could see right through him and into the swamp too.

"Um, Rogr?" Edie shifted from foot to foot, an uneasy smile plastered on her face.

Rogr's ghost blinked and he nodded. "I thought I heard Alfnil calling for me."

"Alfnil?" Pickett whispered.

Edie elbowed her gently and whispered, "Northfellow. Obviously."

Obviously.

Pickett cleared her throat. "Well, you just missed him."

Rogr's face fell. "Oh. Do you know where he went?"

Pickett jerked a thumb over her shoulder at the burning pyre. Rogr frowned at her for a long moment before his jaw dropped open.

"Oh no." He breathed. "I am too late."

"I dunno. Maybe." Pickett shrugged. "But if you want to catch him, you probably ought to go. He's been dead a few hours."

Rogr looked like he might say something—or at least burst into tears. Instead, he clenched his jaw, gave a tight nod, and faded into the dark night.

A full minute passed before either of them moved. Edie plopped down onto the ground where Rogr had been just a moment before, bunching her hands in her skirt.

"Good fuck," Edie breathed.

Good fuck indeed.

"Come on," Pickett said. "Let's go home. I need a drink."

CHAPTER

TWENTY-FOUR

Of course, Edie insisted they couldn't leave until the pyre was down to embers because they might light the trees on fire and burn down some local village. So Pickett took that as a chance to hunt down the shoe she'd removed and plop down into the mud to catch a quick nap. When Edie woke her, the first warm rays of yellow sun pierced through the haze. Within an hour or two, it would start cooking the rotting dead around them, and the infamous stink of the Rottering swamp would become legendary.

As she walked, the pain from Pickett's wounded heel climbed through her whole foot. Then her shin and calf. Then her entire leg. And one foot squished far more than the other. Even without the curse or whatever it was the Northfellow had inflicted on the swamp, some things remained painfully obvious. Wounds didn't just heal magically. If anything, magic was a fucking problem for people like her to survive.

She could only hope whatever kindly or at least less-fucking-awful god was looking after Edie would incidentally protect Pickett too. Edie stopped periodically to give Pickett a chance to catch up as she limped slowly along the boardwalk. And all

170

along the way, the recent dead kept popping up, dead eyes and scales and claws floating out along the surface, bouncing off of old logs.

"What do you bet people start covering their noses before we see them again?" Pickett laughed. Then froze.

Because Edie had frozen, staring forward with wide, horrified eyes, her mouth hanging open.

Edie turned back slowly. "Pickett," she whispered.

But Pickett didn't need an explanation. As she limped up to Edie's side, she saw it. There was the Pick's Pocket in all its shabby glory. And, nearing it, a mob of perhaps a dozen people. A third of them carried torches. Half of the rest carried whatever implement they must have assumed would make a difference. Pitchforks. Shovels. Oars. All of which could be deadly to a couple of women defending their home.

Pickett squeezed Edie's shoulder. "Right," she breathed "This might be a problem."

"Looks like the Swamp Witch act just backfired."

Yes, it did. But it would be fine. It had to be fine. Pickett squared her shoulders, took a deep breath, and marched forward.

Slurne stood at the front of the mob, because of course he did. He started at Pickett's approach, then brandished a trowel like it was some sort of sword.

"You!" he snarled. "We want you gone. Get your things and leave or so help me—"

Pickett shoved her shoulder right into his gut, sending him flying into the filthy waters. As he sputtered, she turned to face the crowd. She had no weapons. No black powder. Nothing useful on hand. And wouldn't it be funny if Fistic didn't get to take the bar from her after all, because her own patrons did it first.

Not that she'd just lie down and let it happen.

"All of you have one chance to leave," she bellowed.

And the crowd bellowed right back.

"We want you gone!"

"Poisoning the swamp!"

Edie darted forward, holding her hands up. "Friends! That's enough. Can't you see the dead went back to being dead? That was Pickett's doing."

"After she raised them in the first place." Deggir pointed a shovel at her, but didn't step any closer.

Pickett had to stop herself from rolling her eyes. Well, she couldn't blame an idiot for not realizing he'd been told the truth. It was so tempting to shove the bastard into the swamp on top of Slurne.

Edie lowered her hands and squared her shoulders. "You're not hurting her," she said, a steely edge creeping into her voice. "And we aren't leaving."

Slurne gripped the edge of the boardwalk, coughing and spitting as he tried to haul himself up. Pickett slammed her heel down on his fingers, sending him back down into the water.

Deggir didn't even glance down at him as his lip curled. "You're either with her or you're with us, kitchen girl." He jabbed his shovel at her. "I'd think carefully about what you choose."

Pickett almost stepped forward. Even if she didn't have any of her tricks at her disposal, she could break his nose. She could rip up a rotting plank and knock him upside the head. But she stopped herself. Edie stared hard at him, then planted her hands on her hips. This was the girl who'd fled her captor and, when she was forced to fight, killed him. Who was Pickett to rescue someone who didn't want it?

Edie raised her chin. "I'm not the one who needs to be careful here." She stepped forward, pressing until the tip of the shovel pressed into her bodice. Deggir's eyes widened just a bit, and he took a step back. Edie followed, pressing against the shovel again.

"You saw what I was willing to do last night when someone threatened my home." She leaned forward, gripping the handle of the shovel as she glared straight into Deggir's eyes.

The would-be mob behind him began to squirm, sharing glances before they backed up.

"I . . . You . . ." Deggir stammered.

"With. A. Kitchen. Knife." Edie narrowed her eyes. Then, quick as a snake, she jumped back, ripping the shovel out of his hands and hoisting it up. "Imagine what I could do with this."

Deggir staggered back, just as Slurne joisted himself up onto the boardwalk. The two collided, and both fell into the fetid waters. Pickett crossed her arms and smirked. Not bad.

"You're just a milkmaid," a member of the crowd said.

Edie glanced over her shoulder.

Pickett gestured at her. "Go on," she said. "It looks like you've got this under control."

Edie arched a brow before turning back to the crowd, raising the shovel like a sword. "I am a member of the Death Shadow Assassin's League. And I'll give you this one shot to back off."

Murmurs rose up from the crowd before someone piped up. "I've never heard of the Death Shadows."

Edie cleared her throat and straightened. "We'd make for piss-poor assassins if everyone knew about us."

"Yeah, why do you think there are so many dead bodies in the swamp?" Pickett asked. "She's just one of many. And do you know what a Death Shadow Assassin does when someone comes after one of their own?"

The crowd shuffled back again. Deggir and Slurne treaded water, hurling insults up at her until Slurne let out a screech.

"Something just touched my leg!"

"It was a bit of swamp grass," Deggir snapped, even as he began to paddle slowly away. "Pull yourself together."

It wasn't a full retreat. Not yet. They needed something to really drive the point home. Pickett scrambled to think of something. Anything. No powders. No flints. What could she do to spook them off?

As it turned out, the answer was absolutely nothing. The door behind her creaked open and the bounty hunter appeared in the doorway. Huh. Some part of her had assumed he'd cut and run.

He locked eyes with her, and raised the crossbow.

"Shit!" Pickett hissed and lunged for Edie, knocking them both to the wooden boardwalk.

A bolt sang overhead before burying itself in a plank just in front of them with a *thunk!*

"If you idiots want a witch, an assassin, and a bounty hunter on your asses," he called out. "Then by all means. Keep this up. I could use the target practice."

Edie scrambled to her feet and raised the shovel for emphasis, and the crowd dispersed, retreating back down the boardwalks to their respective shitty little villages. Even Slurne and Deggir didn't try to pull themselves up. Especially not when a scaly snout popped up out of the water, fixing a sharp, yellow eye on them. Deggir and Slurne screamed and splashed away. Pickett had to laugh.

"Muriel?"

She could swear the swamp beast gave her a little wink with one translucent eyelid and, unable to stop herself, Pickett dropped down to her knees and patted the monster right atop her armored head. Muriel closed her eye and growled softly in a way that almost sounded like a purr.

"Good girl. I take it Hoag sent you?"

There came a grunt and Muriel disappeared back below the water. Was that supposed to be her keeping an eye on them or thanking them for protecting the swamp and, by extension, her clutch? Not that it mattered. As far as those miscreants knew, the swamp witch had a swamp beast protector.

"Thanks, girl!" she shouted as the beast disappeared off into the gray waters.

Pickett turned back and had to stare. Behind her, a swamp beast headed home to her master. Before her, she had a bounty hunter she'd been ready to kill and the kitchen maid she was supposed to protect as *her* defenders.

And still, she couldn't help glaring at the bounty hunter.

"Where's Letterboy?"

He scowled and gestured at her with the crossbow. "I'd have thought you'd have a word or two of thanks."

"All right. Thanks. Where's Letterboy?"

The bounty hunter rolled his eyes but glanced back behind him. "Sleeping. Last night wore him out."

That was a relief. Edie held out a hand and Pickett took it, staggering to her feet. "Do you expect a tip or would you consider sticking up for you part of the payment from last night?"

"Neither." The bounty hunter shrugged. "You put a lot of effort into helping a kid. I respect that."

Oh. Pickett blinked and glanced at Edie, then back at him. "That's-that's a pretty low bar for respect."

"Some would go lower." Fair enough.

Pickett nodded and stepped toward him. "In that case, thank you. Properly. You're welcome to bunk here anytime. Just don't, you know, encourage patrons to turn on me while the dead rise."

The bounty hunter narrowed his eyes but smirked as he gripped her hand. "Don't tie me up and I won't need to."

"Well I think proper introductions are in order." Edie elbowed Pickett gently as she stepped forward. "This is Pickett. I'm Edaneth, but you can call me Edie."

"What?" Pickett frowned. "Edaneth? Really?"

Edie's smile turned brittle. "Yes, but I prefer Edie."

"All this time and you never told me your name?"

"And you never told me that a man was going to come in and try to take all of our money to pay your debts." Edie crossed her arms. "I still come out on top."

Fair enough.

The bounty hunter chuckled and clipped his crossbow back in place. "Well, Pickett, Edaneth. I'm Jodiah Becker."

Jodiah. Pickett bit her cheek as Edie shot her a warning glare, silently warning her not to make fun of the man with the crossbow.

"Good to meet you." Pickett gestured inside. "Come on. I'll pour you a drink."

"Hold the bibblewood juice." He stepped aside to let her through but frowned. "You know your foot is bleeding?"

What else was new?

CHAPTER

TWENTY-FIVE

T he first day back, Pickett didn't remember much more than little flashes, like half of a story that never made it to its own conclusion. She remembered walking into her absolute trash pile of a bar. Past the table that had been pushed over the hole in the floor and a few holes that hadn't been there when she and Edie had left. Clearly Letterboy and Jodiah had suffered their own adventures while she and Edie had been gone. The moneybox was gone. Some of the scant wall art had been ripped and ruined. One of the only things that remained the same was the Northfellow's chair, right where he always came to it. Right where he'd never come again.

And right around then was where Pickett wanted to neither feel nor think about any of it for a very, very long while. She went behind the bar, grabbed one of the remaining bottles of rum, and got to work. At some point, Edie dug up what remained in the larder. Potato shims gone greasy and hard tack that needed a good soak before it could be eaten. She vaguely recalled Jodiah complaining about the potential for scurvy, because they didn't have a single piece of fruit in the bar. But she was pretty sure he ate.

Letterboy came down eventually, and at some point he showed off his scabbing finger to Edie. The poor kid was crying. He must have really thought he was going to lose it. Pickett tried to pour him a drink to celebrate, but Edie wouldn't let her. Apparently in backwater towns like Gallraven, children weren't allowed to so much as touch a spirit, even when they had something to celebrate.

After that, it was all a fog. Pickett woke with a terrible headache, her face pressed against a sticky spot on the floor. The reek of the swamp wafted through one of the holes next to her. Huh. Someone must have pushed her near it in case she was sick in the night. There was also a bottle of already boiled water next to her.

With a groan, Pickett pushed herself up, wobbling for a moment. Her stomach churned, and she couldn't quite decide if she was going to be sick. When nothing came up, she decided it was safe to have a drink of water and look around.

This place had once been a fishing shack. She'd built on the back room, added the stage and the bar, and brought in tables and scraps she could call art for the walls. She'd bought mugs and glasses and rum and beer. She'd created a myth to protect herself and trusted in fate.

That was her biggest mistake. When had fate ever been kind to her? If she thought about it, she'd never been close to earning what she needed to pay Fistic back. She'd just had hope that things would turn around. Hope that, eventually, one wild plan or another would be the one she could use to drag herself up out of this hole.

With a sigh, she took another deep pull of water, deep enough that her head spun and she coughed some of it back up, through the hole into the water.

"Good to see you're finally up," Edie called, poking her head in. "I'm soaking some tack. We need full stomachs before a long day of work."

Pickett blinked blearily before pushing herself to her feet. The whole bar spun around her, but by this point in her life she had enough experience not to respond to it. She waited for it to stop, then puttered into the small kitchen. In the corner, Letterboy was still curled up in the bedding. Pickett frowned.

"Where's the bounty hunter?"

Edie shrugged. "Jodiah said he had business. I feel like he's going to be something of a stray cat."

A stray bounty hunter. Just what she'd always wanted.

They spent the better part of the day puttering about and doing what they could to get the bar put back together. But it was slow going. There were multiple holes in the floorboards, broken doors, and shattered chairs. Even if they could somehow miraculously summon a crowd of customers, Pick's Pocket was in no fit shape to serve them. They were screwed.

Halfway through the afternoon, there came the familiar sound of squeaky wheels and a lovely singing voice.

> "Oh the stories I could tell you about Paradisal
>   girls,
> And how wonderful it is to touch their Paradisal
>   curls."

Pickett groaned and rested her head on the bar.

"Edie, send him away. I haven't got any money for him." Nor customers to serve that rum to. She wanted very much to curl up into a self-pitying ball and sulk until Fistic sent a fresh enforcer to drag her off to servitude.

> "The trouble is the time will come for you to back-
>   ward roam,
> So you'll have to choose between your Paradisal
>   girl and home."

The song ended, and there was a low murmur of conversation. Followed by an exclamation of shock and dismay from Kellum. It was good Edie was here. Pickett didn't presently have the capacity to deal with feelings like this. Idly, she considered digging around for another bottle of rum, getting drunk, and giving up on putting the bar back together when Edie returned.

"Kellum dropped off the rum," she said. "He'll be back later."

"Huh?" Pickett turned and peered at Edie through a haze of frizzy curls. "You told him we can't pay for the rum."

"I did."

"You told him the bar is in ruins."

"He saw."

"You told him we've scared off half our clientele and the moneylender's going to take this place and drag me off to servitude, leaving everything to rot without me."

Edie snorted and settled on a chair. "You're being dramatic. I'll still be here, after all. And apparently, so will Kellum."

Pickett groaned. "There'll be nobody to perform for."

"Wrong. He can perform for us. But we need to at least finish patching these holes so he doesn't fall into the swamp." Edie hopped to her feet and gave Pickett a sharp swat on the rump. "Come on. Work to do."

CHAPTER

TWENTY-SIX

It was so tempting to consider taking the rum and running. Maybe she could sell it in one of those villages bordering the Rottering swamp to make a little money. She could cut her hair, adopt a new name, and disappear. It was a nice fantasy, but she doubted it would work.

They finished what repairs they could. At least enough to reasonably ensure nobody would accidentally plunge in the swamp walking from one corner to the other. When Letterboy finally did wake, it was with complaints of hunger. Edie dug through the rum bottles and found that Kellum had left behind a bag of jerky and a rind of cheese along with his cart, so the three of them split the meager meal, during which Pickett gave him the abbreviated explanation of the night's events. At least she told him what she wanted him to believe.

The Northfellow lost his mind and used magic to poison the swamp. Pickett summoned great and magnificent magic of her own to return the dead back to their grave and summoned a god to carry the Northfellow to eternal rest.

Afterward Pickett sent Letterboy along to wherever he

needed to be next, because she didn't have any more food for him.

"We could try fishing again," Edie suggested as they watched him go. "If the magic's really gone from the swamp, the fish might be good again."

Pickett wrinkled her nose. "Even if that is the case, there's a lot of bodies rotting down there right now. I'd rather wait until the swamp filters some of it out before I try it again."

Edie arched a brow. "So you're considering the possibility that we'll last long enough for that to happen?"

She really did have a nasty habit of digging through every awful situation to try and find a small sparkle of hope.

Pickett heaved a sigh. "I will allow that it's not on me alone. Whatever happens, this is your bar too."

Edie beamed and slipped her hand into Pickett's. "No more secrets?"

"None concerning this dump." Pickett knocked her uninjured heel against the wall. "But we're still in trouble. Fistic's not a man you run from and he's going to want his money back. If we can't earn it the old-fashioned way . . ." She swallowed and squeezed Edie's hand. It felt like jumping off a bridge, but knowing the water was deep enough to protect her from the rocks. "If he indentures me, do you think you'd be all right on your own?"

"Of course. I'm not just your kitchen maid anymore. I'm a master assassin now." She pulled her hand free and flicked Pickett's nose. "And no more trying to protect me. Clearly, it only causes problems."

Pickett laughed with her master assassin of a kitchen maid, a fitting companion for a swamp witch con artist.

"Well, master assassin. Care to kill a bottle of rum with me?"

Edie hummed and headed back into the bar. Unfortunately, there would be no rum, but rather boiled water and what remained of the jerky. Food would be a problem. They'd have to work out something to trade if they wanted to eat for the next few days. Pickett was halfway through a scheme when a fresh knock sounded at the door. And in came Kellum, along with a dozen unfamiliar men, cast in the golden glow of dusk like they'd been sent by the gods themselves.

Pickett gawked as they stepped gingerly inside, glancing around like they thought the walls might bite them, but Kellum marched forward, his chest puffed out.

"These lads are from the *Traverser*," he explained. "They're on shore leave for the next week. I told them they could get free drinks if they were willing to do some repairs."

Edie clapped with delight, but Pickett shook her head.

"Listen, boy, we can't even pay you for the rum."

"You will," he said. "I'll just take the whole of my tip hat until it's paid off."

It had to be a trap. There had to be more of a catch. But as some of the sailors pulled out helpings of hard tack and cheese, Pickett's stomach growled.

"All right," she said reluctantly, and Edie began directing them to their duties.

TWENTY-SEVEN

A s far as crowds went, it wasn't bad. Sure, Pickett had sacrificed far too much rum to the sailors repairing the bar, but it was a relatively small price to pay for a bar that was actually safe to visit. There were no more holes in the floor. More than that, they had actual doors. And somehow, she wasn't sure how, they'd managed to banish the perpetual swamp funk from the wood. Maybe they'd let some of their friends know to come later.

Pickett nibbled on a bit of hard tack, made less hard by Edie's careful efforts. She didn't understand how Edie had become such an expert cook. But here she was, turning an old fishing shack into a place worth visiting.

Up on the stage, Kellum twirled in Romona's old skirts, earning whooping hollers and applause from the audience of sailors. It drowned out half the lyrics sure.

> "Oh do not tell the washer wench
> Her tongue is free as a bird
> But every secret she may spill
> Will twist to the absurd."

There were customers in her bar. They were buying drinks. They were buying tack, albeit cheaply. They were filling her moneybox however slowly. It was a good night so far.

Until the door opened to an unwelcome client.

"Oh fuck," Edie hissed.

Pickett narrowed her eyes as Slurne shuffled in, shoulders slumped. He headed for the bar and made to take the Northfellow's old seat. Pickett glared at him. He backed away.

"I-I was wondering if maybe, if I could—"

"Feeling sorry for yourself because your friend is dead and you tried to run me out of the swamp?"

He ducked his head. "Until that new road is built and there's an establishment there, this is the only place around."

"You're not welcome in any of the villages, are you?" Edie said dryly.

She gripped the rough, wooden handle of one of their knives, but Pickett rested a hand on her wrist.

"You see this bar? This bar is now full of sailors who beat on ropes and drag on heavy sails all day every day. They don't know you. If I told them about you, they wouldn't like you. They like me."

Kellum gave a bit of a saucy twirl in that moment, sending those very sailors whooping and cheering as they sloshed beer. One punched his friend in the arm hard enough to send him sprawling to the floor in a fit of laughter. Funny. The sailors were better behaved than the fishermen.

Slurne nodded morosely. "I understand."

"And from now on, you'll pay double the price for your drinks."

"Ulp!" He blanched, but Pickett removed her hand from Edie's wrist and he hurried to nod. "U-understood."

"Lovely. Edie, if you'd be so kind."

Edie wasn't kind about it at all as she haphazardly splashed some rum into a cup and shoved it at Slurne, spilling some onto his trousers.

Pickett grinned at her and, in that moment, everything felt a bit steady. Yes, doom was coming. But it was still a little ways off. As Kellum settled on the stage with his mandolin and started playing a slower, gentler song, a curious peace settled in Pickett's chest. It would be all right. Whatever happened, Edie would be all right. Probably. Pretty certainly. And the bar would continue operating. Pickett didn't have to take care of everything herself.

"You know," she said softly. "I'm not a dancer. But maybe I could try."

Edie beamed and took Pickett's hand.

"I could show you."

"I'd like—"

The door opened again. Pickett swore if it was another one of those heinous pricks who'd tried to run her out, but it wasn't. It was Letterboy leading a man in a fine waistcoat with a pewter ring on his finger. Gods' taints, she couldn't even get one good night, could she?

"You've got to be kidding me," Edie muttered, but Pickett held up her hand.

"One of us has to play nice," she pointed out. Well maybe not nice, but she could at least play not-homicidal. And maybe this was their new unwritten agreement. Pickett would stop lying to Edie to protect her. In turn, Edie would trust Pickett to act first, even if that hadn't worked every time before.

Unless she was completely misunderstanding things between them. But she hoped not, because Edie sighed and nodded, which probably meant she wasn't about to do anything stupid—especially not in a bar full of sailors who could take them out as easily as they could Slurne or anyone else. Pickett made her way to the end of the bar, where the enforcer stood, his expression stern and unreadable. Was that how Fistic chose them? Did he just wander out and offer a job to anyone who looked intimidating.

"Evening," she said airily. "What can I get you?"

The enforcer grunted and reached into his waistcoat, pulling out what looked like a letter.

Letterboy jumped up. "Wait, I want to give it to her!"

He snatched the letter from the stoic enforcer's hand and slammed it down onto the bar with a toothy grin. Did the kid not realize that this letter was going to be a bad thing?

"Letterboy, maybe you should go to Edie," Pickett suggested. "She'll have a crust of bread for you."

"No. I wanna see." He leaned so far forward in the chair that he was practically laying on the bar amidst the dirty cups and glasses. He'd have a good view of everything going to hell.

Pickett's gut wriggled as she turned the envelope over, seeing the wax seal of the schooner with three coins. It would be all right. It had to be all right. She and Edie had talked it over. Fuck. She wanted to throw the letter in the enforcer's stupid blank face and run for her life. Instead, she forced herself to break the seal and tug out the letter.

The top of the page was filled with all sorts of legal nonsense Pickett couldn't decipher, all written out in Fistic's familiar handwriting. Something about her initial loan. The bar. Interests and accruals and whatever the fuck escrow was.

And then . . .

In light of the bequeathal of the liquid assets and holdings within Southfen belonging to Alfnil of the Troll coast, the remainder of the debt on the aforementioned establishment known as Pick's Pocket is reduced to only 25 percent of the principal investment.

Assets? What in every heaven or hell was this talking about? Letterboy positively bounced in his seat.

"The Northfellow told me to do it a month ago," he said. "If anything happened to him, he wanted all his fortune to go to you. He said it was because you were so nice to him."

"Idiot. I'm not nice to anyone," Pickett muttered, her words strained around the sudden lump in her throat. A month ago. That must have been when he planned to do this. So even from the start, he knew it might kill him and he'd planned for it. Was she really the only person in his life he could leave this to? And how did a batty old drunk have this much money?

"Maybe he was talking about Edie," he said with a shrug. "But he said he wanted to make sure I took care of it and I did!"

"You sure did, kid." Pickett grinned and reached under the bar for a bottle of rum, but Edie appeared in an instant, slapping her wrist and snatching it back.

"Don't you dare." She hissed, but Pickett grinned and held out the letter.

"Come on. The kid did good. Our money troubles are over, well lessened."

"Eh-hrm!"

The enforcer cleared his throat and made a circling motion with one finger, a silent gesture for her to go on.

She snatched back the letter and skimmed it further until . . . Oh.

"*In light of the unknown whereabouts of an employee of one Hurb Fistic, the remainder of the debt is to be closed upon immediately,*" Pickett read, her heart sinking a little lower with every word. "*Failure to produce the necessary funds will result in the seizure of the primary asset and a one-month period of indenture or a retention of said assets for an indenture period of three months with return upon successful completion of the contract.*"

Damned if she did. Damned if she didn't. Either way, she'd be sent off far from Pick's Pocket to serve a mystery master. She should have fought harder to stop the death of that damned enforcer.

Then again, three months wasn't exactly three years. Certainly not long enough for her to be sold to a pirate-hunting vessel. And if she could survive the night in a swamp with the living dead, maybe she could survive this.

Edie's hand wrapped around her forearm, grounding her back in the moment.

"It's your bar, Pickett." She reminded her. "But it's my bar too. You're not the only one who loves it."

Pickett took a deep breath and nodded. Surely Edie could keep the place safe for just three months.

Up on the stage, Kellum put away his instrument and started reciting bawdy jokes.

"When a soon-to-be-widow took too long in giving birth to her first child, her husband poked his head in. The midwife told him the baby had not yet crowned so he suggested she check her backside, as sometimes he took that route. It was a pity the poor babe never knew his father."

The crowd laughed. A crowd of happy customers just a few months away from having a legitimate place. A place one patron had appreciated so much, he'd bequeathed all that he had in an effort to help it stay afloat. What must this place have meant to him? What might it mean to so many others?

She wasn't the only one who loved it. She also wasn't the only one responsible for it anymore.

Pickett glanced back at Edie, her heart in her throat. "If I hand the bar over to you, I'll be gone three months. Can you handle that?"

Edie smiled and nodded. "It'll be here when you get back. Just one condition." She held out her hand. "One dance before you go."

Pickett grinned and took it.

"Just the one."

ACKNOWLEDGMENTS

I'd like to thank Kevin Pettway for creating this incredible universe, as well as the partnership between Ann Rose and Kelly Colby. It's a pairing a hell of a lot sweeter than bibblewood juice and rum!

About the Author

C.M. McGuire may or may not be a cryptid living in central Texas, spoken of only in hushed whispers in small circles. It is said she holds degrees in history and creative writing and, when away from her word processor, teaches. This can only be corroborated by her elderly dog and 2 cats, but thus far they are tight-lipped.

JOIN THE CURSED DRAGON SHIP NEWSLETTER

Love what you just read? Want more just like it? Sign up for our newsletter so you don't miss out on the adventure. You'll get:

- A free book for signing up
- Advanced notice of new releases
- First word of books on sale
- Opportunities for free books
- Most up-to-date information on author appearances.

We're busy and know you are too. We won't send more than one newsletter a month.

Register below.

CHECK OUT THE SERIES THAT STARTED IT ALL

Stealing the cash box of your mercenary unit as you run away probably isn't wise, but it sure is funny.